THE DOCTOR'S BABY DARE

MICHELLE CELMER

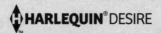

Special thanks and acknowledgment are given to
Michelle Celmer for her contribution to the
Texas Cattleman's Club: Lies and Lullabies miniseries.

ISBN-13: 978-0-373-73439-9

The Doctor's Baby Dare

Copyright © 2016 by Harlequin Books S.A.

Never Too Late
Copyright © 2006 by Harlequin Books S.A.
Brenda Jackson is acknowledged as the author of this work.

Recycling programs
for this product may
not exist in your area.

Printed in U.S.A.

CONTENTS

Michelle Celmer is a bestselling author of more than thirty books. When she's not writing, she likes to spend time with her family and their menagerie of animals.

Michelle loves to hear from readers. Like her on Facebook or write her at PO Box 300, Clawson, MI 48017.

Books by Michelle Celmer

Harlequin Desire

Black Gold Billionaires

The Caroselli Inheritance

Texas Cattleman's Club: Lies and Lullabies

Visit her Author Profile page at Harlequin.com, or michellecelmer.com, for more titles!

THE DOCTOR'S
BABY DARE

Michelle Celmer

One

Dr. Parker Reese considered himself an all-around great guy.

He was affable and easygoing and had a great sense of humor. He was also honest and respectful and always willing to lend a hand. He was a rock in a crisis and a natural born leader. And despite the fact that he'd lived in Texas for only three months and knew nothing about cows, he had just been accepted into the prestigious Texas Cattleman's Club. And they didn't let just anybody in.

Parker was one of those rare individuals who got along with everyone. Everyone who knew him liked and respected him.

Well, almost everyone.

Parker glanced across the hospital cafeteria to the table where the object of his recent fascination sat eating her lunch, phone in hand, earbuds in place to deflect any unwanted attention. Head nurse of the new pediatric ward at Royal Memorial Hospital, Clare Connelly was smart and competent, by far one of the best nurses he'd ever worked with. She ran a tight ship on her ward, and was highly regarded by her coworkers.

And for reasons that escaped Parker, she refused to like him.

Lucas Wakefield, chief of surgery and fellow Texas Cattleman's Club member, set his tray down on the table and dropped into the seat across from Parker. "Mind if I join you?"

Parker grinned. "I think you just did."

If it wasn't for Luc, Parker wouldn't even be in Texas. The two had met at a conference when they were both medical students. At the time, Parker had been working toward a career in cosmetic plastic surgery for the rich and famous, the only medical field his father considered lucrative enough for a tycoon's son, and one that Parker knew would never elicit any real sense of pride. As was often the case, his father's own selfish demands and archaic values trumped Parker's happiness.

Luc had told him to screw the old man and convinced Parker to follow his true passion. Pediatrics. And for the first time in his life Parker stood up to his father. There had been a fair amount of shouting, and threats to cut Parker off financially. His father had even threatened to disown him, but Parker told him that was a chance he was willing to take. His father finally, though reluctantly, conceded. That put an end to the threats and manipulations his father had always used to control him, and for the first time in his life, Parker felt truly independent. But the event had caused a fissure in their relationship, one that took many years to heal. Even so, by the time his father had passed away last year, they'd managed to resolve most of their differences.

After a lifetime of coveting his father's approval, he'd earned it. And now, with his inheritance, Parker had the means to do anything he wanted, wherever he wanted. He knew that he needed a change, that the only reason he'd stayed in New York was to be near his ailing father. Aside from his practice, and a few good friends, there was nothing tying him there. He knew it was time to move on. But where?

Enter Luc. He'd called out of the blue to offer Parker a job in the town of Royal, Texas. Dr. Mann, Royal Hospital's neonatal specialist, was retiring and they were looking for a replacement. The salary wasn't all that impressive, but Parker's inheritance left him set for life. So he sold his practice and relocated to Texas.

Best move he ever made.

"So, did you ever call that girl you met in the gift shop?" Luc asked, dumping a packet of sugar in his coffee.

"We had dinner," Parker told him.

"And..."

"Then I took her home."

"Your home or hers?"

"Hers."

"Did she invite you in?"

They always did. And he didn't doubt that the next stop would have been her bedroom, and a couple of months ago he wouldn't have hesitated. But something about it, about all of his romantic relationships lately, felt hollow. "She invited, I declined."

Luc made a noise like he'd been punched in the gut.

"Dude, you're killing me. I'm married and I'm having more sex than you are."

At thirty-eight, the ever-widening age span between Parker and the twentysomethings he'd been dating was losing its luster. What he was looking for now was an equal. Someone to challenge him. He glanced over at Clare again. Someone capable of stimulating his intelligence as well as his libido.

Luc followed Parker's line of sight and rolled his eyes. "Dude, let it go already. How many times have you asked her out?"

Parker shrugged. He'd honestly lost track. A couple dozen at least. At first her rejection was firm, but polite— for the most part. Not so much anymore. Lately he could feel the tension when they were forced to work together. Which was often. But that was okay. It would just be that much more satisfying when she gave into him. And she would. They always did.

"What do you think it is about me that she finds so offensive?" he asked Luc.

"Could it be your inability to accept *no* as an answer?"

Parker shot him a look. "She wants me. I guarantee it."

He glanced over at her again. Her eyes were lowered, but she knew he was looking. He wasn't sure how he knew, he just did. He could feel her from across the cafeteria. In her early thirties, she was nearly a decade older than the women he typically dated, but he liked that.

"You really can't stand it can you?" Luc said and Parker turned to him.

"Can't stand what?"

"That she won't bend to your will."

It would irritate him a lot more if he didn't know that it was temporary. But yes, he was used to women falling at his feet. And honestly, it wasn't as great as it sounded. "Clare will change her mind. I just have to catch her at the right time."

"When the chloroform kicks in?"

Parker laughed in spite of himself and said, "Let me tell you a story. When I was a kid, there was a girl at my school named Ruth Flanigan. And for reasons unknown to me, Ruth relentlessly picked on me."

"You were bullied by a girl?" Luc laughed. "Is that some sort of ass-backward karma?"

"It's funny now, but at the time it was traumatic. She would shove me in the lunch line or kick my shins on the playground. She pulled my hair and knocked me off the swings. For years I was afraid of girls."

"Clearly you got over that."

Had he? Sometimes he wondered. When it came to relationships, he was always the one calling the shots, the one in control. He only dated women who were substantially younger and intellectually inferior. That had to mean something.

"So, what happened?" Luc asked him.

"At some point in the second grade she either moved or switched to a different school. I don't remember exactly. I just remember coming back to school in the fall, and being relieved that she was no longer there. I didn't have any contact with her again until college. I was home for the holidays and I ran into her at the party of a mutual friend."

"Did she kick your shins?"

"No. She confessed that she'd had a huge crush on me, and torturing me was just her way of showing it."

"Don't tell me you're going to kick Clare in the shins and pull her hair."

"Of course not." Though he was sure the hair-pulling part would come later, if she was into that sort of thing. "My point is, just because someone acts as if they don't like you, it doesn't mean it's true."

"Are you seriously suggesting that Clare is only *pretending* not to like you?"

Parker shrugged. "It's not impossible."

"You clearly have your pick of female companions. Why this infatuation with Clare?"

Because she fascinated him, and not just because she was the only woman he'd ever met who was seemingly immune to his charms. Weird as it sounded, he just felt drawn to her. He wanted to crack her open, peek inside and see what made her tick. Metaphorically speaking of course.

Clare had been on the hospital staff for almost a decade, but Parker had yet to find a single person who knew her on a deeply personal level. Which he thought was weird. He spent far more time with his coworkers than anyone. He liked to think of them as extended family. But then, he had always been a very social person. Clare was not. She always sat alone in the cafeteria, and kept to herself on the ward. He'd heard that she had never been married or had kids, and had lived with her old-maid aunt since college. But like the librarian who wore sexy lingerie under a conservative and drab suit, Clare had layers, and boy would he love to be the one to peel them back. He was sure he would find sexy underthings in there somewhere. He was betting that if she wanted to, Clare could teach him a thing or two about having fun.

"I'd just like to get to know her."

"I've never known you to fixate on a woman this

way," Luc said. "I have to say it's a little disconcerting. It's like you're obsessed."

He had no explanation for why he felt such a deep connection to Clare. In the past he'd avoided deep connections like the plague. Why this time did it feel so…natural?

He knew her work routine like the back of his hand. Knew exactly when she started her rounds, when she ate her lunch, when she worked on charts. He knew her smile, and the melody of her voice, though when she used it to address him it was always filled with irritation. But he was getting close, he could feel it.

Okay, maybe he was a *little* obsessed.

"Even if you're right," Luc said, "and she doesn't hate you as much as she lets on, everyone knows that Clare doesn't date coworkers."

"There's a first time for everything," Parker told him. "And I never say never."

"I think that's your biggest problem."

Luc could poke fun all he wanted—Parker was confident he would wear her down. "I give it a month, probably less."

With a sly grin that said he was up to something, Luc asked, "Are you willing to bet on that?"

"You'll lose," Parker told him.

"If you're so sure, put your money where your mouth is."

It wouldn't be the first time they had entered into a friendly wager. "The usual amount?"

"You've got a deal," Luc said and they fist-bumped on it.

Parker's phone rumbled and he pulled it from the pocket of his lab coat. It was Vanessa, a nursing assistant from the NICU.

"I'm sorry to bother you, Doctor, but we need you up here. Janey's vitals are erratic again."

He cursed under his breath. Born premature and abandoned on the floor of a truck stop, Baby Janey Doe had been brought into Emergency last month and had instantly captured the heart of everyone on the ward. And though she was getting the best medical care available, her little body just wasn't ready to heal.

"Be right there," he told her, then rose, telling Luc, "Gotta go."

"Janey?" Luc asked, and when Parker nodded Luc shook his head grimly. "No improvement?"

"It doesn't make sense," he said, gathering up what was left of his lunch. "I've run every test I could think of, scoured the internet and medical journals for similar cases, but nothing fits. I'm at a loss. In the meantime her little body is shutting down. I'm worried we might lose her."

"It sucks, but you can't save them all."

He knew that, and he'd lost patients before. "Maybe I can't save them all," he told Luc, "but I'll never stop trying."

Clare Connelly sat in the hospital cafeteria, headphones in, wishing this day would hurry up and be over. This morning when she'd gotten into her car, it had stalled several times before she finally got it running. Then it had stalled again at a red light when she was halfway there, and she'd wound up with a line of angry drivers behind her. As she'd pulled into the hospital lot the skies had opened up and dumped a deluge of rain on her as she walked to the building.

Yesterday had been their monthly family dinner at

her parents' horse farm an hour away, and though she had warned them that she might have to work, apparently Clare's absence had caused a stir again. Her phone had been blowing up all morning with calls from her seven siblings. When her brothers or sisters missed dinner no one freaked out. Of course, they all saw each other on a regular basis.

Her three brothers and two of her sisters worked on the farm, and her other two sisters were stay-at-home mothers with four children each. In total Clare had twenty-two nieces and nephews ranging in age from newborn to twenty-six. It seemed as if every time she turned around one of her siblings was expecting another child, and her oldest niece and nephew were both newly married with first children on the way. An entirely new generation to remind Clare how much of a black sheep she really was.

Being single and childless in such a traditional family made her a target for well-meaning and sometimes not-so-well-meaning relatives. No one could grasp the concept that she actually enjoyed being single, and that she wasn't deliberately going against the grain. She was just trying to be happy on her own terms. Refusing to join the family business after high school had sent relations into a tizzy; they'd tagged her as the rebel. If they had bothered to pay attention they would have known she had always dreamed of being a nurse. But from the day she graduated from nursing school they had teased her relentlessly, saying that she'd only entered the profession to snag a rich doctor and live in a mansion.

Her gaze automatically sought out her new boss.

An attractive, smooth-talking multimillionaire well-known for his philanthropy, Parker was every woman's dream. With his *GQ* model physique, rich brown hair always in need of a trim and eyes that looked green one minute and brown the next, he was way above average on the looks scale. Way, *way* above. At the sight of him on his first day at the hospital, her female staff had been reduced to giggling, blushing, hormonally driven adolescent girls.

He was hands down one of the finest physicians she'd ever worked for. He was trustworthy, honest, reliable, and she had never once seen him in a foul mood. He was as charming as he was funny, and his often rumpled, shabby-chic appearance only added to his appeal. And despite being an East Coaster, he had exceptionally good manners. But most important, his rapport with children made him an outstanding pediatrician.

He was also a shameless, womanizing serial dater. Or so she had heard. One who had apparently set his sights on her.

As if.

She'd learned the hard way that emotional entanglements with a coworker, especially one in a position of power, were a prescription for disaster. It was how her no-dating-coworkers rule had come to be. And though she'd made every effort possible to ignore him, he made that nearly impossible with his relentless teasing and barely veiled innuendo. All of that unwanted attention had resulted in a mild crush.

Mild crush? She nearly laughed out loud at the understatement. She could fool her family and her coworkers, but she couldn't fool her own heart. And though she would die before admitting it to another human being, she wanted him. Badly.

Getting that first guilty glimpse of him every morning, with his slightly rumpled hair and lopsided tie, was by far the highlight of her day. She would imagine brushing back that single soft curl that fell across his forehead and straightening that tie and then she would push herself up on her toes...

And that was where it always ended because if she let herself go any further, she would forget all of the reasons she needed to keep him at arm's length. But even if he wasn't her boss, he was off-limits. If her family got wind that she was dating a doctor, especially a rich one, they would never let her live it down.

She just wished he would stop *watching* her. He had her so tied in knots she could barely eat her lunch. She supposed that was one of the advantages of a crush, or lust, or whatever this thing was. Inevitable weight loss. Since Dr. Reese had moved there, Clare had dropped a total of eighteen pounds. She hadn't been this skinny since her first year of college. She felt so good without the extra weight that she'd begun jogging again. Though she did realize she would have never put on those eighteen pounds in the first place if she hadn't gotten lax with her exercise regimen. Then again, she'd had no one to look good naked for. Nor the time or even the desire to go out and find someone.

In her peripheral vision she saw Dr. Reese rise from the table where he'd been sitting with Dr. Wakefield, and her stomach did a flip-flop. He would have to walk past her to leave the cafeteria. Keeping her eyes on her phone, she watched in her peripheral vision as Parker neared her table, and when he walked past she could feel the air shift.

Would he stop and give her a hard time? He was always making excuses to talk to her about things that weren't work related. Probably because he knew it annoyed her. That's what she wanted him to think anyway.

Parker must have been in a hurry because he didn't stop this time. She should have been relieved, so why the feeling of disappointment? She couldn't go on this way, harboring an irrational lust for a man who was completely wrong for her, walking around in a state of constant confusion.

Her phone rang and she answered, instantly back in work mode when Vanessa, one of her nurses, told her Janey's vitals were no longer stable and getting worse by the minute.

Clare jumped up, leaving her tray on the table and shoving her phone in her cardigan pocket as she headed for the closest elevator. Since she'd been discovered in the truck stop, just minutes after her birth and barely clinging to life, Janey's condition had been touch and go. Being in the medical field, Clare had been trained to put her personal feelings aside and remain objective, but Janey was like no other patient she'd ever had. She had no one, and despite efforts to find her family, or anyone who may have known who her family was, the police had come up empty, so Janey had become a ward of the state. Clare couldn't imagine being so helpless and alone, nor could she understand how a woman could abandon her child that way. Though she had no children of her own, or plans to have a baby anytime soon, Clare could see how fiercely protective her sisters were of their children. What could have happened to Janey's mom to make her think that her baby would be better off without her? Or maybe she hadn't been given a choice.

The idea gave Clare a cold chill.

She rounded the corner to see the elevator doors sliding closed and broke into a run, calling, "Hold the elevator!"

A hand emerged to stop the door, a hand that she realized, as she slipped inside, was attached to the very person she was trying to avoid. And now she was the last place she wanted to be.

Stuck alone with him.

He hit the button for the fourth floor, wearing a look that made her knees weak, and as the doors slid shut said, "Hey there, sunshine."

Two

Clare shot Parker one of those looks. This one seemed to say, *Seriously, did you really just call me that?*

But a month ago she would have completely ignored him, so that was progress. Right?

"They called you about Janey?" he asked her.

"Erratic vitals," Clare said, her concern for the infant clear on her face. Janey had made an emotional impact on everyone in the NICU, but Clare seemed more attached to her than anyone. He couldn't deny that Janey's case had tested his objectivity from the minute she was admitted to the hospital, barely clinging to life. And now, with treatment options diminishing, he was feeling the pressure.

There had to be something he was missing…

"She's not getting better," Clare said as if she were reading his mind.

"No," he agreed. "She isn't."

A code blue was called over the PA for the fourth floor. Parker looked at Clare, and she looked at him, and they cursed in unison. Their fragile patient had gone from unstable to arrest.

Knowing it wouldn't do a bit of good, he stabbed the button for the fourth floor again. Janey could be dying and the two people responsible for her care were stuck on a damned elevator.

"If this thing moves any slower I'll have to get out and push," he told Clare.

It felt like an eternity before the elevator dinged for their floor. They stood side by side, like sprinters at the starting line. The instant the doors slid open they broke into a run. By the time he reached her, Janey was in full cardiac arrest. Nurses stood around watching anxiously as a pediatrics resident performed manual CPR on her pale and limp little body. The sight of it was so heartbreaking Parker had to dig down extra deep for the focus to perform his duties.

"Let me through," he barked, and a group of startled staff instantly cleared the way. He never raised his voice to his team, or anyone for that matter, but this was bad.

"She's not responding," the resident said as Parker took over the heart compressions.

"Call her cardiologist," he barked to no one in particular, knowing someone would do it.

He tried to find a pulse, and couldn't. "Come on, little one. Fight for me."

He continued the compressions to no avail.

Damn it, he had hoped it wouldn't come to this. "Paddles," he said, turning to his left where Clare always stood, surprised to find a different nurse there.

He glanced around and found Clare standing *way* over by the door. Her face looked pale and her eyes wide, and for an instant he was sure she was about to either be sick or lose consciousness. Unfortunately he had a sick infant who took priority.

Even using the paddles it took almost thirty minutes to get Janey stable, and afterward everyone breathed a huge sigh of relief, including him. She was okay for now, but that had been a really close call. He turned to find Clare, who he had assumed wouldn't leave Janey's side for the reminder of her shift, but she was gone.

He texted her, checking the hallway as he waited for an answer, but after several minutes the message was still tagged as unread. Clare always read and answered her messages.

He frowned. Something was definitely up.

Assuming she'd gone back to the nurses' station, he headed that way. "Have you seen Nurse Connelly?" he asked Rebecca, the nursing assistant sitting there.

"She walked by a second ago." She looked up at him through a veil of what he was sure were fake lashes. "So, I was thinking we could get together again this weekend."

Oh, no, that was not a good idea. He liked Rebecca, but she was a party girl and these days he could barely stay awake past eleven thirty. His father used to tell him, *You're only as old as you feel.* After a night of partying with Rebecca and her friends, he felt about eighty. She was fun and sexy, but the inevitable hangover wasn't worth it. He could no longer stay out till 3:00 a.m. then make it to work by seven and still function. He was pushing forty. His party days were over.

He checked his phone but still no text.

"Did you see where Nurse Connelly went?" he asked Rebecca, ignoring her suggestion completely, which she didn't seem to like very much.

"Sorry, no," she said tartly.

He doubted he would be getting any more help from her. Ironically, this very situation was probably why Clare didn't date people from work. A lesson he clearly hadn't learned yet.

So, where the hell had she disappeared to? Did she go back down to the cafeteria? Had she slipped past Rebecca and gone to the elevator? No, he thought with a shake of his head. Knowing Clare, she wouldn't want anyone to see her lose her cool, so where would she go for guaranteed privacy? At the end of this hall there was a family waiting room—the last place she would go—and the door to the stairs…

Of course! That had to be it. He'd taken a breather or two in the stairwell himself. Or used it to sneak a kiss with a pretty young nurse. She had to be there.

He found Clare sitting on a step halfway between the fourth and fifth floor, arms roped around her legs, head on her knees so her face was hidden.

"Here to harass me in my moment of weakness?" she asked without looking up.

"How did you know it was me?"

"Because that's the kind of day I've been having." She lifted her head, sniffling and wiping tears from her cheeks with the heel of her palms.

Tears?

Clare was *crying*?

Just when he thought she couldn't be more interesting, or perplexing, she threw him a curveball.

"And I know how your shoes sound," she added. "From hearing you walk up and down the halls."

He would be flattered that she paid attention, but she paid attention to everything on the ward.

"Are you all right?" He offered her one of the tissues he kept in his lab coat pocket. He dealt with parents of sick children on a daily basis. Tissues were a part of the uniform.

She took it and wiped her nose. "I'm okay. Just really embarrassed. I don't know what happened in there."

"You choked," he said, knowing Clare would want an honest answer. "It happens to the best of us."

She lifted her chin stubbornly. "Not to me it doesn't."

If she had been standing, and was a foot taller, he was sure she would be looking down her nose at him. "At the risk of sounding like a tool, all evidence is to the contrary, cupcake."

Outraged, she opened her mouth, probably to say something mean, or respond to the *cupcake* remark, then something inside her seemed to give. Her face went slack and her body sort of sank in on itself. She dropped her head to her knees again, groaning, "You're right."

He was? She really *must* have been out of sorts because she never thought he was right about anything.

"Are you okay?" he asked.

"You know those days when you feel like you could take on the world? When everything goes exactly the way you want it to?"

"Sure."

She looked up at him with red-rimmed, bloodshot eyes. "This is not one of those days."

He cringed. "That bad, huh?"

She dropped her head back down to her knees. "Choking on the job is just the icing on the cake."

Clearly. "So you really never choked?"

She shook her head, making her messy bun flop from side to side, and said, "Not even in nursing school."

He took a chance and sat down beside her. She didn't snarl or hiss, or unsheathe her talons, so that was good. "Is there anything I can do?"

"Shoot me and put me out of my misery."

"I think you're being a little hard on yourself," he told her. He had heard of surgeons who choked during surgery and never got their confidence back, but this was different. This wasn't a matter of confidence, this was pure human emotion.

"What if it happens again, when she *needs* me?" Clare said, looking up at him. She had the prettiest eyes, and she smelled amazing. It would barely take anything to lean in and kiss her. Her lips looked plump and delicious. It might even be worth the concussion afterward, when Clare clocked him.

"If there hadn't been fifteen other people in the room to compensate, if it had been just you and me, or even just you, I have no doubt that you would have performed admirably," he said.

"It's getting more difficult to be objective with her," Clare said, looking genuinely distraught. "When they called the code I thought for sure that this was it, that this time she wouldn't snap back. It made me sick inside, like she was my own flesh and blood."

"Your compassion is what makes you such a good nurse."

"Yeah, I'm awesome," she said. "I was so limp with fear I barely made it out of the elevator. I was sweating and my heart was pounding and I felt like I couldn't breathe, and all the way down the hall it was like I was walking through quicksand."

It sounded like a panic attack, but to suggest it would probably only make her feel worse. "These are special circumstances."

"How do you figure?"

"Until they find Janey's mother, or get her into foster care, you and I are the only 'parents' she has. She may be a ward of the state, but it's up to us to see that she gets the best care. That's a huge responsibility."

"You're right," she said, sounding cautiously optimistic. "Maybe that's why I have this deep need to protect her."

"Right now, she needs protecting."

She looked up at him and there were those lips again. Plump and juicy and pink. She had pale, flawless skin and the brightest, clearest green eyes that he had ever seen.

He would never forget the day he'd met her, when she'd walked into the staff meeting and the administrator had introduced them. He had been totally blown away. He'd probably held her hand a little too long when he shook it, and all through the meeting he hadn't been able to stop staring at her. Which, in retrospect, might have seemed a little creepy. Maybe they'd just gotten off on the wrong foot.

"I'm not sure if I've ever said it, but you're a really good doctor," she said.

He wiggled his brows and said, "Flattery will get you everywhere."

"Now if we could just do something about your personality," she grumbled with an exasperated shake of her head, but there was the hint of a smile, and a twinkle of something sly and impish in her eyes. She was teasing him.

"Admit it," he said, teasing her right back. "I'm starting to grow on you."

"I admit nothing," she said, nose in the air, trying not to smile, but he could see that she was having as much fun as he was. "Though I will say that after this, it might be a little more difficult to dislike you."

He grinned and wiggled his brows. "Then my evil plan is working."

Clare laughed. She couldn't help it. Because it was just so *Parker*. And boy did it irritate her that she knew him well enough to say that. Five minutes ago she'd felt lower than low; now he had her laughing. How did he do that?

Try as she might to push him away, he always pushed back a little harder. Was this campaign to keep him at arm's length a futile waste of time? Was falling for him an inevitability?

She refused to believe that. She would just dig extra deep for the will to resist him.

No meant no, not maybe.

"You know that I don't date people from work," she said. "Especially doctors."

He grinned. "Who said anything about dating?"

The way he was looking at her mouth... If only he knew how tempting that really was.

On second thought, it was probably good that he didn't know. "I don't sleep with people at work either," she said.

"We definitely won't be sleeping. And we won't be

doing it at work." His grin was teasing, but there was a fire in his eyes, and it was one hell of a blaze. He was so damned sexy and he smelled so good. He'd missed a small strip of stubble on the underside of his chin. Any other man would look sloppy or unkempt. On Parker it looked sexy and charming. And she wanted to kiss him there. And pretty much anywhere else.

Okay, *why* was she saying no? He had a body to die for; he was beyond gorgeous. Not to mention nice, with a really good sense of humor, and she had the feeling that he would not disappoint in the bedroom. Maybe, if they could keep it a secret…

No, no, no!

What was wrong with her? She was a strong, independent woman. When she made up her mind about something, there was no changing it. So why this sudden ambivalence? What was it about being around this man that made her go all gooey?

The dynamics were fairly simple: rich doctor, bad.

Parker was watching her, looking amused. "Penny for your thoughts."

Considering the semismug grin he wore, her inner struggle must have been pretty obvious.

Swell.

"Tell you what," he said. "Since you seem to be having a rough time with this, I'm going to give you an easy out."

Why would he do that?

Suspicious, she asked, "What's the catch?"

"No catch. If you can *honestly* tell me that you aren't attracted to me, and that you want me to leave you alone, I promise I'll back off."

Really? After all this time he would really just give up? "I'm not attracted to you," she said.

His smile was smug. "That was great. Now tell it to *me*, cupcake, not your shoes."

Darn, she was hoping he wouldn't notice the lack of eye contact. The truth was, she was a terrible liar. As a child she could never get away with anything.

There was no avoiding it—she had to look at him, and the instant their eyes met, she was totally tongue-tied. He seemed to know every button to push and he pushed them liberally. But that was what womanizers did, right?

"You *are* evil," she said.

"Nah, just irresistible." He stood and held his hand out to give her a boost. "We'd better get back on the floor before someone misses us."

Without thinking, she took his hand, realizing as he pulled her up how insanely stupid it had been. Though they bumped elbows and shoulders occasionally, other than a handshake when she met him, they had never deliberately touched each other. And while she didn't actually see any sparks arcing between them as his hand wrapped around hers, boy did she feel them. And so did he.

"Interesting," he said, with a slight arch of his brow. "*Very* interesting."

That single word spoke volumes. But mostly it just told her that she was in *big* trouble.

Three

Her arms loaded with bags of donated clothes, Clare trudged through the brisk February wind to her car in the staff lot. It had gotten so cold the puddles of rain from earlier that day had turned to patches of ice. All she wanted now was to go home, take a long hot shower, crawl into bed and forget today ever happened. Although mostly she just wanted to forget the part with Parker.

Janey had begun to show very slight signs of improvement over the course of the day, but she was nowhere close to being out of the woods. Fragile as she was, her condition could turn on a dime. Until they could figure out what was wrong, they were treating the symptoms, not the cause.

Clare left the night staff very strict instructions to contact her if Janey went into distress again. She wasn't obligated to come in on her off hours, but this wasn't about obligation. And hopefully it wouldn't come to that.

Shivering, Clare popped the trunk, dropped the bags inside and then unlocked her car with the key fob and slid onto the icy-cold seat. Shivering, she stuck the key into the ignition and turned...

Nothing happened.

"Are you kidding me?" she grumbled.

She tried again, and again, but the engine was dead.

She got out, pulling her collar up to shield her face from the icy wind. She popped the hood and looked at the engine for anything obvious, like a loose battery wire. She'd watched her brothers work on cars her entire childhood and she had learned a thing or two. Her car was almost fifteen years old and malfunctioned from regular wear and tear. She had been planning to look for a new one next month when the weather was better, but it looked as if she might have to do it sooner.

With her aunt away for a week she really had no one to pick her up. She would just have to call a tow truck and wait around. Hopefully it wouldn't take long.

She dialed the garage and was informed that they would be there ASAP. Which meant no more than an hour.

"I'm supposed to wait in the freezing cold for an hour?"

"Just leave your keys in the glove box."

Grumbling to herself, she hung up. Now she would have to call a cab to get home. But she would do it inside the hospital where it was warm.

She put her keys in the glove box and shut the door.

She was getting ready to close the hood when she

heard a vehicle pull up behind her car. She knew before she even heard him call out to her who it was. Because that was the kind of day she was having.

"Looks like you could use some help, angel face."

There he was, in his sporty import, grinning at her. She wanted to be exasperated but she couldn't work up the will.

"Car's dead. I called for a tow."

"Need a lift?"

It sure beat waiting for a cab, though she knew she was asking for trouble. But she was exhausted and frustrated and she just wanted to get home. "If it's no trouble."

Oh, that smile. "Hop in."

"Can I put something in your trunk?"

"Is it a dead body?"

She opened her trunk. "Well, not the whole thing."

He grinned and popped his trunk. "In that case, absolutely."

She tossed the bags inside, closed the trunk and climbed in the passenger's side. The interior was soft black leather and her seat was toasty warm.

She took off her gloves and held her hands in front of the heat vent.

"Where to?"

She told him her address, and how to get there, but as he pulled out of the lot he went in the opposite direction. "Hey, genius, my house is the other way."

"I know. But dinner is this way."

She blinked. "Who said anything about dinner?"

"I just did. If I don't eat something soon I'll go into hypoglycemic shock."

"You really think I'm going to fall for that?"

His grin said that she didn't have a whole lot of choice.

Damn it. She should have known better than to get in his car. But she was too exhausted to argue. She let her head fall back against the seat rest.

"You can't tell me that you're not hungry. I know for a fact that you didn't get to eat your lunch."

Of course she was hungry. She was starving, but he was the last person she wanted to be seen with in a social setting. The way gossip traveled in the town of Royal, people would have them engaged by the end of the week.

"No offense, but I really prefer that we not be seen together outside of work."

"So, not only do you not date coworkers, but you don't dine with them either? Is that why you always eat lunch alone?"

"That's not why I eat alone, and no, I have nothing against dining with coworkers. It's just something I don't do often."

"So then having a meal with me shouldn't be a big deal, right?"

She was pretty sure he already knew the answer to that question. And as he pulled into the parking lot of the Royal Diner, the number one worst place to go when trying to avoid the prying eyes of the town gossips, she found herself wishing that she'd called a cab instead.

"I can't risk someone seeing us and getting the wrong idea."

"We're just two colleagues sharing a meal while you wait for a tow. Not to mention that I'd like to talk about Janey. Bounce a few ideas off of you. Think of it as an offsite work meeting."

Well, if it was a work meeting…

"Just this one time," she said. "And I mean that."

He grinned, shut the engine off and said, "Let's go."

Since he was the type of guy who would insist on opening a car door for a woman, she hopped out before he could get the chance. And when he reached past her to open the diner door, she grabbed it first. She didn't want anyone getting even the slightest impression that this was a date.

The hostess showed them to a booth near the back. It was after eight so most of the dinner rush had already cleared out. Which could only be a good thing. "What would you two like to drink?"

"Decaf coffee," Clare said.

"Make that two," Parker told her.

"Enjoy your meal," the hostess said, laying their menus on the table.

As they sat down Parker said, "See, it's not so bad. There's hardly anyone here."

He was right. The subfreezing temperatures must have kept people inside tonight. But it would take only one nosy person to see them together and draw the wrong conclusion.

Their waitress, Emily, was someone Clare knew well. She often brought her autistic daughter to the free clinic on the weekends when Clare was volunteering, and her husband worked at the auto-repair shop. She set their coffees down and Clare didn't miss the curious look as she said, "Hey, Clare, Dr. Reese. Looks cold out there."

"So cold Clare's car wouldn't start," Parker told her.

"Are you still driving that old thing?" Emily asked her.

"I know I need to get a new one," she said, warming her hands with her coffee cup. "I just haven't had time."

"Do you know what you'd like to order or would you need a minute to look at the menu?"

"I know what I want," Parker said, eyes on Clare. From his mischievous grin, Clare knew he wasn't talking about the food.

"Caesar salad with the dressing on the side," she told Emily.

"Would you like chicken on that?"

Would she ever, but she was only five pounds away from her high school weight and she wanted to hit that number by swimsuit season. "No chicken."

"My usual," Parker told Emily.

"One Caesar, one bacon cheeseburger and fries, comin' right up."

When she was gone Parker said, "She knows what car you drive?"

"Everyone around here knows what everyone drives."

His brows knit together. "That's weird."

Not for Royal it wasn't. "You've never lived in a small town, have you?"

"Nope. I've always lived in the city, but I like the slower pace. Though it has taken some getting used to."

"You must eat here often if you have a usual," Clare said.

"Several times a week at least, and sometimes I come in for breakfast."

"You eat a burger and fries several times a *week*?"

"I'm a carnivore. I eat meat."

"There's this thing called vegetables…"

He shrugged, sipping his coffee. "Sometimes I order a side salad."

He was a doctor, for God's sake. He should have known better. "What do you have the other four days?"

"That depends on who I'm with," he said, and his cheeky smile said that once again they were no longer talking about food. But she'd sort of walked into that one, hadn't she?

Why did he have to be so damned adorable, with his stubbled chin and dark, rumpled hair? The soft waves begged to be combed back by her willing fingers and his hazel eyes smoldered, though they looked more whiskey-colored in this light. He'd loosened his lop-sided tie and opened the top button on his dress shirt…

"Have you lived in Royal your whole life?" he asked her.

Jarred by the sudden change of subject, she realized she was staring at his chest and lifted her gaze to his handsome face instead. Which was just as bad, if not worse. Sometimes when she was sitting at the nurses' station and he was nearby she would watch him in her peripheral vision. He had such a nice face to look at.

"I moved here to live with my aunt about a year after nursing school," she told him.

"Where are you from originally?"

"My parents own a horse farm about an hour from here. Five of my siblings work there."

He blinked. "*Five?* How many siblings do you have?"

"Seven. All older. Three boys, four girls."

"Wow." He shook his head in disbelief. "That's a lot of kids."

"Tell me about it."

"Catholic?"

"No, just very traditional. My mom has six siblings and my dad has four. They both grew up on farms."

"What about your siblings. Do they have kids?"

"As of last month I have twenty-two nieces and nephews, and two great-nieces on the way."

"Wow. That is a *big* family. And you're the baby?"

There was nothing more annoying than being referred to as *the baby* by her family. It was their way of pushing her down and keeping her in her place. But when Parker said it, with that teasing smile, it wasn't demeaning at all.

"I'm the youngest, yes."

"Were you spoiled?"

As if. "My parents were pretty burned out by the time I came along. As long as I did my chores and kept my grades up they pretty much left me alone. I would rather be invisible than get sucked into all the family drama."

"I used to wish that I had a big family."

"Do you have siblings?" she asked him.

"Only child."

"I had a friend in school who was an only child and I was always so envious."

Emily returned to the table with their food and Clare's stomach howled. Though getting a salad had been the responsible thing to do, Parker's juicy burger and greasy fries beckoned her.

"Well, it's not all it's cracked up to be," he said, popping a fry in his mouth, and when he offered her one, she couldn't resist. Her mouth watered as the greasy, salty goodness sent her taste buds into overload.

She looked at her plate, then his, and thought, *Man, I should have ordered a burger.*

"Growing up I always wanted siblings," Parker said, pushing his plate toward her, gesturing to her to take more.

"I had to share a room with three of my sisters. I had no privacy whatsoever." There hadn't even been anyone who'd keep things in confidence. If one sibling knew, they all knew. Because of that it had always been difficult for her to trust people to keep her secrets. Her aunt was the only person in her life she could be totally honest with.

"For what it's worth, I didn't either," he said, and she watched his lips move. She loved looking at his lips. It was always the first place her eyes landed.

"My father was very strict throughout my entire childhood," Parker said. "He controlled pretty much every aspect of my life, like which friends I was allowed to have, what books I was allowed to read. He even chose the classes I took in high school. He was grooming me to take over his business. I always thought that if he had another child he might not be so focused on my every move."

"What does he do?"

"He was a financial tycoon. He passed away last year."

"I'm so sorry."

"We had a very tenuous relationship. I had no interest in finance, and he considered practicing medicine beneath me. He agreed to pay for medical school, but only if I studied to be a cosmetic surgeon. He even set up a job for me with his own cosmetic surgeon when I graduated."

As amazing as he was with children, that would have been a terrible waste. "Clearly you changed his mind."

"It was Luc Wakefield who talked me into standing up to my father."

"How did that go over?"

"There was a lot of shouting and threats. He said

he would disown and disinherit me. I said go for it. At that point I was so sick of being controlled I honestly didn't care."

Her family may have been a ginormous pain, but his father sounded a million times worse. "What did your mom have to say about it?"

"Not much," he said, and his casual reply belied the flash of something dark and sad in his eyes. But as soon as it was there, it was gone again. "She wasn't around."

For whatever reason, she had just assumed that someone as successful as Parker would come from a well-adjusted and happy home. She imagined him as the golden child, probably captain of the football team, valedictorian and loved by all.

It would appear that she was wrong. Again. That's what she got for drawing conclusions without facts.

"Have I got something between my teeth?" Parker asked suddenly.

She blinked. "No. Why?"

"Are you sure? Because you haven't stopped staring at my mouth."

Her cheeks went hot with embarrassment. Was she really doing that?

"It's either that, or you're thinking about kissing me."

She was almost always thinking about kissing him. She really had to be more careful in the future where she let her eyes wander. And her thoughts.

"I don't suppose you played football in high school?" Clare asked, and Parker laughed.

"No, I didn't. But if I had, boy, my father would have loved that." The only thing that would have pleased his dad more than Parker taking over the family business was if he'd become a professional athlete. But it had been obvious from a very early age that Parker had no interest, and more important, no natural talent.

He was barely out of diapers when his father began pushing him into various sports. First soccer, then T-ball, but he'd sucked at them both. He'd been more interested in sitting on the sidelines, searching the grass for bugs and snakes.

His dad had enrolled him in tag football when Parker was six, and had forced him to stay for the entire season. Luckily Parker had had a sympathetic coach who'd let him spend most of his time on the bench. Because as fanatical as his father had been about his son's physical abilities, he'd never once made it to a practice or even a game.

Swimming lessons had come next, but Parker got so many ear infections as a result that the doctor told his father the lessons had to stop. Parker's equestrian training was probably the least horrible thing he'd been forced into, and though being so high up on the horse's back had always made him nervous, he loved animals. Until his horse was spooked and threw him, and nearly trampled him to death. That was the last time he'd ever gone near a horse.

"My father played ball in college," Parker told her. "I guess he just assumed that I would want to play, too. He was real big on me following in his footsteps. He wanted a mini me, and I seriously didn't fit the bill. I was skinny and scrawny and kind of a geek."

"You were not," she said, taking another fry, eyeing his burger with a look of longing. She had barely touched her salad, but she'd already eaten half his fries.

"I'm serious. I was a total nerd. Remind me and

I'll dig out some old pictures." He slid his plate closer. "Take a bite."

She blinked. "Of what?"

"My burger. You haven't taken your eyes off of it, and I think I see a little drool in the corner of your mouth."

She hesitated, looking a little embarrassed, but her stomach won the battle. "Well, maybe a little bite…"

There was nothing little about the bite she took.

"I didn't start to really fill out until my third year of college," he said. "When I started weight training."

"So you were what, like, twenty-one?"

"Eighteen. I graduated high school when I was fifteen."

"Wow, you really were a geek. But your dad must have been happy about that."

"My dad was never happy about anything. He was a tyrant. Thankfully I saw more of the nanny and the house staff than him."

"I went through sort of the same thing when I was a kid. Although not the tyrant part. Everyone assumed I would work on the ranch after high school, but I wanted to be a nurse. I knew from the time I got my first play doctor kit as a kid that I wanted to work in medicine. I wanted to help people."

"Did you ever tell your family that?"

"Probably a million times, but I was more or less invisible. No one ever listened to what I had to say. Hell, they still don't. If it isn't ranch business, or my various nieces' and nephews' academic accomplishments, they don't discuss it. So I worked my butt off in school and got a scholarship to a college far away from home and haven't looked back since. My parents were not very happy with me."

In what universe did that make even a lick of sense? "Aren't most parents proud when their kids go to college?"

"Like I said, they're very traditional. Nothing was more important to them than their children 'paying their debt to the family,'" she said, making air quotes with her fingers. "Whatever the hell that meant. I didn't ask to be born. I never felt as if I owed my family anything."

It amazed him that despite their very different upbringings, their childhoods weren't really all that different. "I felt the same way about my father. He had my entire life planned out before I was out of diapers. With no regard whatsoever to what I might want. But that was just who he was. People were terrified of him and he used that to manipulate. No one dared deny him anything."

"Stubborn as I am, my parents' archaic thinking probably only pushed me further from the fold. The thought of staying on the farm and working with my family for the rest of my life gives me hives. And they have no respect for what I do. To this day I still hear snide remarks about going into medicine just to snag—" She stopped abruptly, but it was already too late. He knew exactly what she'd been about to say.

"A wealthy doctor?" he said.

Her cheeks flushed a deep red and she lowered her eyes to her salad, her juicy bottom lip wedged adorably between her perfect teeth. He'd never seen her blush, but damn, she sure was pretty when she did. But then, she always looked good to him. And suddenly her attitude toward him made a whole lot more sense.

"I didn't mean to tell you that," she said, looking mortified.

"At least now I know why you spend so much time pretending you don't like me."

She lifted her chin, getting all indignant on him. "Who says I was pretending?"

He laughed. "Sweetheart, I've dated a lot of women. I know the signals."

She opened her mouth to argue—because she always argued when he was trying to make a point—then must have had a change of heart and closed it again. "Okay, yes, that is *part* of the reason I can't see you. But there are other factors, as well, things I'm not comfortable getting into right now."

"So you do like me," he said.

"I respect you as a physician and peer, and you seem like a good person. I could even see us eventually becoming friends, but it can never be more than that."

Four

"Do you want to be friends?" Parker asked her.

She wanted that and so much more, and it wasn't fair that she couldn't have it. But she of all people knew that life was not often fair. She also realized that neither of them had said a word about Janey. Not that it surprised her. It was all just a ruse to get her alone. And she'd fallen for it. Willingly. She looked at her phone to check the time. "It's late. I should go home. I want to get up early tomorrow and go jogging."

Her very obvious brush-off didn't seem to faze him. "You don't strike me as the jogging type."

"I like it. There's a cute little park behind my house."

"Are you one of those die-hard joggers who's on the road before the sun's up?"

"God, no. If I'm on the track at seven thirty it's a good day."

He just grinned and said, "Could you be more intriguing?"

She didn't even know how to respond to that. She led a pretty unexciting life. What did he see that was so special? So interesting? If he was just looking to get laid, he was seriously overplaying his hand.

Parker motioned Emily for the check, and refused to let Clare pay her portion.

"You can buy next time," he said, but she didn't think there was going to be a next time. It was stupid to think that she could ever be friends with Parker without wanting more. *So. Much. More.* So she figured, why tempt herself? Out of sight, out of mind. Wasn't that the way it was supposed to work?

"Where to?" he asked when they got into the car. He blasted the heat and switched the seat warmers on.

"We're just outside of town. Turn left." Thankfully this time he followed her directions.

"Didn't that area get hit pretty hard by the tornado?" he asked as he pulled out of the parking lot.

"Our house was leveled," she said, realizing that she could look at his mouth all she wanted now; he was focused on the road.

"Tell me you and your aunt weren't in the house," he said.

"My aunt was away on a trip and I was at the hospital."

"Were you able to salvage anything?"

"We lost everything. Clothes, furniture, keepsakes. My aunt travels extensively and she had things from all over the world. Things she'd been collecting for decades. By the time it was over, they were scattered all over the city. Wet and broken. My aunt's file cabinet, with the papers still in it, was found over a mile away. The tornado picked her car up and launched it through the house across the street. It was utter devastation."

"I can't even imagine," he said. "I've seen some major hurricane damage on the East Coast, but nothing that bad. And you saw it? The tornado, I mean."

She nodded. "It was surreal at first. I kept thinking that it couldn't happen to Royal, that at the last second it would change course or blow itself out, then the debris started to hit things. Windows started breaking and cars in the hospital lot were getting pummeled with softball-sized hail and we knew we were going to be right in the middle of it. You feel like a sitting duck. All you can do is take shelter, hang on tight and hope for the best."

"The hospital has a shelter, right?"

"Yes, but I wasn't in it. It happened so fast, there was no time to move the patients, so, along with the rest of the staff I stayed on the ward."

"That was very brave."

"No." She shook her head. "I was terrified. It was the longest five minutes of my life."

"You were terrified but you did it anyway. You put the lives of those kids before your own. That's the definition of bravery."

The compliment, coming from him, made her heart go pitter-pat. Why did he have to be so nice? And so ridiculously handsome? Did the man have a single negative attribute? Other than being extremely stubborn. But to be fair she was guilty of that, too. He turned into her subdivision and took a right onto her street.

"It's the third house on the left."

"You know, I've learned more about you tonight than in the past three months," Parker said.

"There isn't much to know. The tornado aside, I don't lead a very exciting life."

"Excitement is highly overrated. And believe me, I'm speaking from experience. I love the slower pace here. The people are so different, so much more laid-back. For the most part. It's exactly what I needed."

It was all about perception, she supposed, because for her this was just normal. But she was sure that moving from Royal to somewhere like Dallas, or even New York City, would be a jarring change of pace. But she never would. She was a country girl at heart and that would never change.

He pulled into the driveway and the automatic outdoor lights switched on, illuminating the exterior of her aunt's sprawling colonial. "This is nice."

"Thanks. It's pretty much identical to the old one, just a little more modern."

"It's a lot of house for two people."

"My aunt has out-of-town guests frequently, so she likes the extra space." She gathered her purse and gloves and said, "Thanks for the ride. And dinner."

"I'll help you with your body," he said, shutting off the car.

She blinked. Oh, man, if he only knew the things she wanted him to do to her body. Sexy, tantalizing things…

Uh-oh, was she drooling a little again…?

She must have looked confused, because he said, "In the trunk. The body bags."

Oh, right, she would have completely forgotten and left them there. "I can get them," she said.

"Nonsense, I'll help." He popped the trunk open and got out of the car. She met him around back.

"Did you really just say *nonsense*?"

"Isn't that how people talk in Texas?"

"If you're eighty. And a woman."

"My bad," he said, but he was grinning. Did the man ever stop smiling? No one should be that happy that much of the time.

She reached for the bags but he snatched them up first. Darn it, the last thing she wanted was to let him into her house. She had the feeling that once she did, it would be near impossible to get him back out the door.

"I've got it," she said, but he was already heading up the walk. Her exasperated breath crystalized in the air as she jogged to catch up. She had no choice but to go along with it. And of course there was a small part of her that wanted him in her house. Or maybe not so small.

"I think you have a hearing problem," she told him as they walked up the porch steps.

"No, I hear you just fine," he said, waiting for her to unlock the front door. "I think what you mean is that I have a *listening* problem."

She laughed; she couldn't help it. "If I say I've got it from here, and it's been a long day and I'm tired, is there *any* way I'm going to stop you from coming in?"

He considered that for several seconds then shook his head. "Probably not. I'll just make up some lame excuse like needing to use the bathroom and we both know that you're too polite to say no."

He was right. Damn those pesky Southern manners her parents had drilled into her. She couldn't decide if it was more disturbing or pathetic that she had little to no ability to deny him anything. Like the tornado, he'd blown into her life and had the potential to make a huge mess of things.

"You could have the decency to look a little less smug," she said, pushing the door open and letting him inside.

"Kidding aside, I really would like to discuss Janey's case," he said, stepping into the foyer, which led into the open-concept great room and kitchen. "We didn't get a chance at dinner."

As if she would say no to that. Besides, this time he sounded sincere, and less like he was trying to get into her pants.

She wondered what he would do if she invited him up to her bedroom. There was no point pondering the possibility, as it would never happen. Not in this lifetime anyway. But it was the kind of thing that she liked to think about. When she was alone. Usually in bed. If he was as good as her fantasies…

No man was as good as the fantasy. She had pretty high standards when it came to casual sex. Her philosophy was simple. Why did she need a man around when she could do it better herself?

"I have to make an early start in the morning, so you've got thirty minutes," she said, shrugging out of her coat and hanging it on the coat tree by the door. He did the same, looking even more rumpled than he had at dinner. Since it would be rude not to offer him a beverage—there were those pesky manners again— she said, "I'm going to make myself a cup of tea. Would you like one?"

"I'd love one," he said.

She gestured to the couch, probably the safest place to confine him. "Make yourself comfortable."

She stepped into the kitchen and filled the kettle, then set the burner on high. The stove, like the rest of the kitchen, was a chef's dream. Major overkill considering neither she nor her aunt liked to cook, but her aunt only bought top-of-the line appliances. She bought top-of-the-line everything.

Clare grabbed two cups from the cupboard and set them by the stove, then pulled out a box of chamomile tea. "Do you take sugar or honey?" she asked him, bracing herself for some sort of suggestive innuendo, but he didn't say a word. She turned to him, and realized that he hadn't answered because he was *gone*.

"Where the heck did you go?" she called, and heard him answer from the second floor.

"Up here."

She was fairly sure that his voice was coming from her bedroom. So much for having to actually invite him to her bedroom. He'd found it all on his own.

Did the man have no boundaries? No shame?

She should have known. She never should have turned her back on him. Hell, she never should have let him into her house.

She charged up the stairs to her bedroom. She found him *sitting* at the foot of her bed, looking around the room. It had been a really long time since she'd had a man under, or even on top of, her covers and he looked damn good there.

"What the hell, Parker?" she said, realizing, as his name rolled off her tongue, that as long as she had known him she had referred to him as Dr. Reese. This was her first time addressing him by his first name. It felt a little odd, but also kind of natural.

He flashed her a toothy smile. "Hey there, short stuff."

At five-five she was hardly short, but she let it slide. "What do you think you're doing?"

"You said to make myself comfortable."

"I meant on the couch."

"But you didn't *say* the couch."

"I pointed to it!"

"Clearly I don't take direction well. You're going to have to be a little more specific next time."

Next time? After this did he seriously think she would let him back in?

Who was she kidding? Of course she would.

She folded her arms. "Get off my bed."

He grinned. "You didn't say please."

"*Please* get off my bed," she said, feeling a little desperate. The urge to jump in there with him was almost too strong to fight. She felt a little winded and tingly all over, as if her libido had just awakened from a long hibernation.

"No need to shout," he said, pulling himself to his feet and walking to the door.

"I don't like having people in my bedroom. I like my privacy." She straightened the covers where he'd been sitting. They were still warm from his body heat, and the slightest hint of his aftershave lingered in the air.

She turned to him to say that it was time for him to go, but he wasn't there!

"Are you kidding me?" she mumbled. "Parker!"

She found him in her craft room next door. He'd switched the light on and was examining the quilt samplers she had sewn and tacked to the wall. "Oh, my God, are you for real? Did I not just say that I like my privacy. You have the attention span of a *three-year-old*!"

"You said you don't like having people in your bedroom. This isn't your bedroom, is it?"

She didn't justify that one with a response. And her thin-lipped glare only seemed to amuse him further. "The truth is, I just wanted to hear you say my name again. Or shriek it, as the case may be."

She ignored the warm shiver that whispered across the surface of her skin and raised the fine hairs on her arms. Or tried to at least. He wasn't making it easy. "I'll say it a thousand times if it will make you go downstairs."

"These are fantastic," he said, gesturing to the wall. She wasn't buying it. He was the kind of guy who knew quality when he saw it and this was definitely not quality sewing.

"Compliments won't get you anywhere," she told him.

"I'm actually serious," he said, leaning in closer. "Where did you get them?"

"I made them, and for the record, they suck. The fabric is puckered and the rows are crooked. My stitching is totally uneven. Which is why I keep them in here. Where no one will see them."

"But the colors are striking," he said, and she realized that he really wasn't bullshitting her. He was genuinely impressed.

Weird.

"You have a gift," he said.

"It's just a hobby. It relaxes me."

"Did you do these drawings, too?"

He was looking at the pages she'd laid out on her craft table.

"I couldn't draw my way out of a paper bag. I just

colored them in. It's the new big thing in stress relief for adults."

"Coloring?"

"Absolutely. There are like a million adult coloring books to choose from."

"No kidding. It seems a little…pointless."

"That's the whole point." She gestured to a pile of coloring books on the shelf beside her craft table. "I've finished all of those. I did a lot of coloring in the park last summer. And look how calm I am."

"Yeah," he said with a wry smile. "You looked pretty calm in the stairwell today."

Of course he would point that out. But it was hard to get angry when he was flashing her that adorable grin.

"May I?" he asked, nodding to the pile.

No one had looked at her coloring books before. It had never even occurred to her to show them to anyone. "Go ahead, but they're nothing special."

He took the top book, a panoramic foldout of a magical fairyland. "Wow, you sure do have a way with color."

The compliment made her feel all warm and squishy inside. "I just pick what looks right."

"That's the weird thing. Normally these colors don't even go together, but you make it seem like they do."

She shrugged, thinking he was making a way bigger deal about this than he should be. "Maybe I wasn't clear. You can rave all you want and I'm still not going to sleep with you."

"You should frame some of these," he said, looking through a book of flowers, ignoring her completely. Or, knowing him, he was only pretending to. She had the feeling that he didn't miss much.

"Why?" she asked him. "They're not art."

"No, this is definitely art."

"Okay, but it's someone *else's* art."

"Yes, the shapes are already there, but the color adds dimension. It brings it to life. That's the hardest part."

Maybe, maybe not. Either way, his enthusiasm was giving her warm fuzzies all over the place. Her inability to resist his charms bordered on the absurd.

"How many finished books do you have?" he asked her, flipping through a collection of mandalas.

She didn't even want to go there. "Too many. I don't get out much."

"Me neither," he said, and she gave him a dubious look. "I'm serious."

"That's not how I hear it."

"Keeping tabs on me?"

She was making it sound that way, wasn't she? "Word gets around. You're reputed to have a very busy social calendar."

"When I first got here I was going out pretty frequently. But I was in a new place and meeting lots of new people."

"New women, you mean."

He shot her a sideways glance through the curtain of his unfairly thick lashes, then winked. He actually *winked*. "Be careful, Clare, you almost sound jealous."

Probably because she was. A little.

He moved closer, looking like a tiger on the prowl, his eyes shining with male heat. If this were the wild, he would take her in an instant. And because it was the wild she would be helpless to stop him. He looked as if he was going to kiss her, and she wanted him to.

His eyes locked on hers, he started to lean in, slowly,

cautiously, as if he was expecting her to hit him over the head with something.

Up until today he had been subtle but consistent. He had never pushed, exactly, but he'd made sure that she knew he was around. Something told her now that all bets were off.

Five

$\mathbf{D}$ownstairs in the kitchen the kettle whistled but Clare didn't move. She stood totally still, her eyes locked on Parker's, the energy whirling between them electrically charged. Parker knew that he could have her right now if he wanted to. This was the moment he'd been waiting for, but half the fun of a relationship was the chase. No matter who was doing the running. And call him a megalomaniac, but it would be much more fun if she made the first move. If she came to him.

Just for fun, he dropped his gaze to her mouth. Her chin lifted a fraction and her tongue darted out to wet her lips.

Oh, yeah, she wanted it bad.

"Your water is boiling," he said.

Clare blinked several times, as if waking from a daydream. "Huh?"

"The kettle, it's boiling."

"Oh. I should probably get that," she said, but she didn't move. She was waiting for him to kiss her. He could feel the anticipation, see the throb of her pulse at the base of her throat.

A wisp of dark blond hair had escaped the messy bun she wore, so he reached up and tucked the silky-soft strand back in. Clare's breath caught and her pupils dilated, and as the tips of his fingers brushed the shell of her ear, she leaned into his palm. He realized, with spine-tingling awareness, that this was the first time he'd touched her. They had bumped shoulders or elbows a time or two while treating a patient, and he'd held her hand to pull her up on the steps today. Touching her felt exciting, and a little naughty.

Her skin was just as smooth and soft as he thought it would be, and damn, she smelled good. He knew that if he kept touching her this way the chase would end right here, right now.

He dropped his hand to his side. "You need a push?"

She blinked with confusion. "A push?"

"To get the kettle. I don't think it's going to turn itself off."

"Right, the kettle," she said, peeling her eyes from his, taking a slightly unsteady step back. The truth was, he was feeling a little unsteady himself.

He gestured her through the office doorway, and she shook her head. "Uh-uh. There's no way I'm taking my eyes off you for even a second," she said. "Next thing I know you'll be going through my closet or something. You're too sneaky."

And she was way too much fun.

He went down first, with Clare watching him like a

hawk. When they got to the kitchen, Clare shut off the burner, never once turning her back on him. Not that he blamed her.

"I'm going to head out," he told her.

Her look of disappointment made him smile. "I thought you were staying for tea."

"Watch yourself, Clare, or I might have to assume you like having me around."

"We wouldn't want that," she said, but it was too late. It was written all over her face. "Thanks for the ride home. And dinner."

"My pleasure." And boy, did he mean that. He walked to the door and pulled his wool coat on. Clare met him in the foyer.

"Do you need a ride to work tomorrow?" he asked her.

"I can use my aunt's car until she gets back next week. I don't like relying on other people."

"And you're afraid that someone will see us together and get the wrong idea." Or the right one.

She folded her arms across what he was sure were a perfect pair of breasts. And he would know soon enough. "We never did discuss Janey."

"Good night, Parker."

He winked. "Good night, hot stuff."

Her eye roll was the last thing he saw as she closed the door. Oh, yeah, she was definitely into him. As if there had ever been a question.

Clare lay awake half the night, and the other half she spent dreaming about Parker. It was as if she couldn't escape him, no matter how hard she tried. Not even when she was sleeping. He was starting to get under her skin. And that was a very bad thing.

The absence of any physical contact between them had been her secret weapon, but he'd taken care of that, hadn't he? The warm weight of his palm against her cheek had been unexpected and startling and so erotic that the resulting surge of estrogen had short-circuited the logic pathways in her brain. It was a wonder smoke hadn't billowed out of her ears. She had been positive that he was going to kiss her, then he didn't and she didn't quite understand why.

She got out of bed late, pulling her hair back into a ponytail and dressing in her warmest jogging outfit. According to the weather report she had seen online last night, the daytime high would barely break thirty degrees. She was so ready for spring and warmer weather.

Her breath crystalized and the icy air burned her lungs as she stepped out the back door onto the multi-level deck. She crossed the yard to a gate, which led right to the jogging path.

She was getting warmed up, stretching her hamstrings, when she heard a familiar voice, using a really bad fake Southern accent.

"Fancy meeting you here, ma'am."

Oh, no, not this morning. She turned to see Parker leaning casually against a barren tree in what looked like a brand-new jogging getup.

"God, give me strength," she mumbled, and told Parker, "You *really* need to stop trying to sound Southern. You're not any good at it."

He just grinned that adorable grin, making her a tiny bit weak in the knees.

"What are you doing here?"

"It just so happens that I jog, too, and I'm always looking for a change of scenery. A different path to take. Your description of the park intrigued me so I thought I would check it out."

"I said it was a cute little park. Which word got you? *Cute?* Or *little?*"

Despite her snippy tone he smiled.

"If I asked you to go away, would you?"

Looking apologetic, he shook his head.

Of course not. She sighed and said, "Let's get this over with."

They started down the path toward the pond, Parker huffing along beside her. But gradually he started to fall behind. They were no more than five minutes in, and Parker was gasping for air. She hadn't even broken a sweat.

Then he stopped altogether, and she had to backtrack. He stood hunched over and out of breath, holding his side. "Damn, this is harder than it looks."

Clearly he was not a jogger. And of course she planned to use that to teach him a lesson. "I'll race you to the pond," she said.

"Are you trying to kill me?"

"I'll make you a deal. If you can beat me there, I'll sleep with you."

His stunned expression was the last thing she saw as she took off running, leaving Parker in the dust.

She got to the pond and was using a bench to stretch when Parker finally wheezed his way over. He dropped like a lead weight onto the grass at her feet, red-faced and sucking cold air into his lungs.

She shook her head sadly. "I know eighty-year-olds in better shape than you."

"You really *are* trying to kill me," he gasped.

"You did lie about being a jogger. You sort of asked for it."

"Technically I didn't lie, because starting this morning I plan to be a regular jogger. If I don't die from exhaustion first. Or a heart attack. I don't suppose you have water."

She took the bottle from her jacket pocket and handed it to him.

"Thanks." He sat up, chugging half the bottle.

"Maybe you should head back to the house while I do my laps. When I'm finished I'll make you breakfast. I guess I owe you that much, since I did almost kill you. Not that I was trying or anything."

"Sure you weren't." He pushed himself to his feet. "Can I wait in the house?"

Did he honestly think she would fall for that one again? "Sure. If you can figure out the alarm code."

She took off running again and he shouted after her, "You're really going to make me sit out in the cold? I could freeze to death!"

She waved without turning around, feeling not an ounce of guilt. More than likely he had a still-warm luxury vehicle parked somewhere nearby. There would be no freezing to death for him.

She jogged her usual laps around the park, then just for fun added a few more, pushing herself harder. Maybe if she was gone a really long time, he would get bored and leave.

As if. If it had been possible to shake him off that easily, he would have been long gone by now.

When she stepped through the gate into the backyard,

Parker was sitting on the steps of the upper deck, tapping away on his cell phone. So much for him leaving.

Parker heard the back gate open and looked up from his phone. Clare was cute when she was all sweaty, her hair a mess. "Good run?"

She nodded, only slightly out of breath. "It got better when I ditched you. You were dragging me down."

"Do I still get my breakfast?"

"Yes," she said grudgingly. She opened the back door and disarmed the alarm. "But don't expect anything fancy."

He tugged off his jacket and took a seat at the kitchen island. "Do I at least get coffee?"

She reached over to the coffeemaker and pressed the start button.

She used the term *making breakfast* loosely. What she should have said was that she would warm up breakfast for him. She "made" him one of those individually wrapped breakfast sandwiches out of the freezer.

"Make yourself useful and get the juice out of the fridge," she said, putting the sandwich in the microwave.

He opened the refrigerator. Aside from the juice and various condiments, there were mostly just carryout containers.

He had the distinct feeling that Clare didn't cook, which was fine, as it was one of his favorite things to do. It was a little spooky the way they seemed so perfectly matched. It was like destiny, or fate or some other crap like that.

Serendipity maybe.

She took two glasses down from the cupboard for

him to fill. Then the microwave dinged and she handed him the sandwich. "Bon appétit."

He bit in to find the middle still partially frozen, but the look she was giving him said not to push it. He forced a smile and said, "Delicious."

"As soon as you're finished eating you have to leave," she said.

"Actually, it's my day off. I can stay as long as I want."

She gave him one of those *looks*, and he grinned. Damn, did he love teasing her.

"You look like a grown man," she said. "You even sound like a grown man..."

He grinned. "If it walks like a duck and talks like a duck."

"You're going to make me late for work," she said.

"As your boss, I give you the day off."

"I don't want to take the day off. I actually like going to work."

"That's probably why you're so good at it."

She shrugged. "Well..."

"I'm serious, Clare. I've never seen a more efficiently run children's ward. Your employees respect you. They look up to you. Sometimes they even fear you a little."

She blinked with surprise. "Really?"

"You can be a little intense at times, and intimidating."

She frowned. "I don't want them to be afraid of me."

"They fear your authority, not you personally. You hold everyone to a super high standard. You demand the best performance at all times. They don't like to let you down."

She actually blushed. "I couldn't ask for a better staff."

"They're as good as they are because of you."

"I'm sure you had something to do with it, too. You're incredibly easy to work for. I liked Dr. Mann, but he was incredibly arrogant. He was always right, and God help you if you disagreed with him. Especially in front of a patient. I've seen some really good nurses get fired for challenging his authority. And even if it turned out they were right, he would never admit it."

"Sounds like he had a God complex."

"Don't get me wrong, he was a good doctor. Just not a very good person. I think he got into medicine for all the wrong reasons."

"We all have our reasons," he said.

"What were yours?"

"Mostly to get laid," he said, wiggling his brows. "Chicks love doctors."

"Chicks?"

"That's right, baby. They dig me."

She was trying really hard not to grin. "The 1960s called. They want their slang back."

He laughed and she cracked a smile.

"Your time is up, daddy-o. Make like a tree and leave."

She was funny, too. And really snarky.

Could she be more enchanting?

Figuring he'd hassled her enough for one morning, he slugged back the last of his coffee, and then left.

Parker spent the remainder of the day catching up on his reading. Medical journals mostly. Then he did some online research regarding Janey's case. Once again, he found nothing that fit her symptoms. He finished around nine that evening, more frustrated than ever. Feeling restless and edgy, he headed over to the Texas Cattleman's Club for a drink. Only a few tables in the lounge were occupied; Logan Wade sat at the bar, hunched over a beer. A hockey game played on the television, but he didn't seem to be watching it. He just stared into the beer mug, mesmerized as he swirled the dark lager around and around. Barely a month ago, Logan had taken custody of his twin brother Seth's baby daughter after Margaret, the child's mother, died in a car crash giving birth. Paramedics were able to deliver the baby, who was surprisingly unharmed, but Margaret never regained consciousness. Margaret's mother, in her grief over losing her daughter and believing that Logan was the baby's father, left the child in his care. Logan swore he'd never met Margaret, and a blood test confirmed that he was related to the baby, but not the parent. So it had to be Seth.

Parker took a seat next to him, and Logan greeted him with a very unenthusiastic, "Hey."

The bartender, without prompting, brought Parker his regular, a scotch and soda. "Who's winning?" he asked Logan, but his friend stared at him blankly.

Parker gestured to the television. "The game?"

"Oh, right," Logan said, and then shrugged. "I guess I have no idea. To be honest, I don't even know how long I've been sitting here. Is it possible to sleep with one's eyes open?"

Parker chuckled. "Baby Maggie not letting you get much rest?"

"She's so fussy. Hadley keeps telling me it's normal, but damn…" He shook his head in exasperation. "Don't get me wrong, she's my niece, and I love her, but I really wasn't prepared for this."

"No luck reaching your brother?"

He shook his head. "The navy took the message, but Seth is on a mission. Who knows when he'll get it. If and when he does, there's still no guarantee he'll come back to claim her. I honestly don't know what I would do without Hadley."

Hadley, Logan's new bride, had come to work for him as a nanny, and the two had fallen hard for each other. It seemed as if everyone around Parker was finding their perfect match and settling down. A year ago that would have given him the heebie-jeebies. Now he wanted what they had.

"She's a keeper," Parker said.

The game went to commercial and the station broke in with a special news report. Both men looked up at the wide-screen behind the bar. Janey's picture flashed across the screen with the caption "Abandoned Baby, Mother Found?" Parker sat up straighter, asking the bartender, "Can you turn that up?"

According to the anchor, a truck driver who had been in the lot of the truck stop the night Janey had been found had come forward with a video. While videotaping his rig, he'd caught a glimpse of a woman, now presumed to be Janey's mother, entering the building. They played the clip, which was grainy and difficult to make out clearly.

"Holy shit!" Logan jumped up so fast the bar stool flipped over backward and everyone in the room turned toward the commotion.

"You recognize her?" Parker asked him.

Logan rubbed his tired eyes and squinted at the television. "That looks like Margaret!"

"Margaret? You mean Maggie's mother?"

"Margaret's mother showed me a picture. I'm pretty sure that's her," he said, and asked the bartender for the remote to rewind the clip. He rewound it twice. "Yeah," he told Parker, "I'm positive. That's Margaret."

And just like that Parker knew exactly how to treat his fragile little patient. He laughed and shook his head. Could it really be that simple?

"Call the police," Parker told Logan, pulling on his coat. "I have to get to the hospital."

Stunned, Logan said, "If Margaret is Janey's mother, that means…"

"It means you have *two* nieces."

A look of shock crossed his face. *"Twins?"*

"A simple DNA test will prove it definitively." Honestly, it was a wonder they hadn't put it together before now. "But if I were you I would go home and get some sleep. If they are twins, your life is about to get a bit more complicated."

Six

Clare woke the next morning to her phone ringing.

She sat up and looked at her phone. Of course it was Parker. Who else would call her at *7:00 a.m.*? On her day off?

"Hello," she grumbled.

"You awake?" he asked.

Duh. "I am now!"

"Good. Come down and let me in."

"You're *here*?"

"I have some very good news."

"Fine," she grumbled, tossing the covers off and rolling out of bed. She tugged on her beat-up terry-cloth robe, and still half asleep, trudged down the stairs to the front door.

"Good morning," he said with a smile when she flung open the door.

"It's 7:00 a.m.," she told him.

"I know."

"On my day off."

"I know." He walked right past her without invitation and took his coat off, dropping it over the back of the sofa on the way to the kitchen, acting as if he owned the place.

It took a good minute to notice that he was unshaven and his clothes were a wrinkled mess.

"You look like hell," she said.

He took in her messy ponytail, puffy eyes and ragged old robe. "Look who's talking."

At least she had a good reason. What was *his* excuse? And what man in his right mind would tell the woman he was trying to sleep with that she looked like hell?

She supposed that was what made him so…*Parker*. When he poured on the charm he was tough to resist. But didn't he know that honesty was not always the best policy?

"Did you not go home last night?" she asked, regretting the words the instant she spoke them. She didn't want to know where he'd been. Or whom he had been with.

Grinning from ear to ear he said, "I did not. I spent the night with a beautiful girl."

Because you're not man enough for a real woman? she wanted to say. "And you woke me at 7:00 a.m. on my day off to tell me this? Are you on drugs?"

He shook his head.

"Mentally challenged?"

He just smiled, then he looked toward the coffeepot and sniffed. "What, no coffee?"

Was he kidding? He really *was* mentally challenged.

"*Seven a.m. Day off. Sleeping.* Is any of this ringing a bell?"

"I'll make a pot," he said.

Ooookay. She flopped down on the sofa. "Knock yourself out."

This was her own fault. She never should have let him get in her head. Or her house. But it was too late now. Now that he was here there was no getting rid of him. And she hated that somewhere deep down she didn't *want* to get rid of him.

She let her head fall back, closed her tired eyes and pinched back the migraine building at the bridge of her nose with her thumb and forefinger. She must have dozed off for a minute or two, or maybe ten, because the next thing she knew Parker was waking her, holding a steaming cup of coffee.

"Time to get up," he said, holding it out to her. "Black, one sugar."

She took the cup, grumbling under her breath as she did. It irritated her to no end that after just one shared meal at the diner he already knew exactly how she fixed her coffee.

"Not a morning person?" he asked, sitting down beside her with his own cup.

"Not on my *day off.*" Especially when she'd spent the previous night tossing and turning, and all because of the man sitting next to her.

"So, about that girl…"

"Ugh! Do I really need to hear this?" she said, resisting the urge to stick her fingers in her ears and sing, *Lalalalala.*

"There you go again, thinking the worst of me," he said.

She had to. It was the only way to keep him at arm's length.

"I spent the night at the hospital," he said. "With Janey."

Clare's heart dropped so fast and hard that she felt woozy. She set her coffee on the table for fear of dropping it from her shaking hands. And though she needed to know what happened, she was terrified to ask.

"She's okay," he assured her with a smile, laying a hand on her arm. "She's been improving all night."

Oh, thank God.

The sudden gush of relief had her shaking even harder. "How? What happened?"

"I finally figured out what's wrong. From watching the news, no less."

"So what is it?"

"It's called twin-to-twin transfusion."

She blinked. "But…she's not a twin. And if she is, where is the other baby?"

"Healthy and happy, and living with her uncle Logan."

She gasped. "Baby Maggie? But…"

"Some truck driver filming his rig got a video of Janey's mother at the Lucky Seven truck stop. She was identified as Margaret Garner by several people. Which means that Maggie and Janey are twins—we confirmed it with a blood test. Although she isn't Janey anymore."

"They gave her a new name?"

"Madeline. But they're calling her Maddie."

"Maddie and Maggie. That's cute. But how did we not make the connection?"

"I beat myself up over that all night. They were brought in separately, worked on by two different teams. She was healthy. There was really nothing to connect.

We're thinking that Margaret didn't know she was having twins. I think she had Maddie at the rest stop. She was probably in shock, and losing blood. I'm sure she had no idea she was still in labor when she got back in her car."

Meaning she probably got little to no prenatal care. "If she'd seen an OB-GYN she would have known it was twins and they could have treated their condition in utero."

"But we both know that it doesn't always work that way. And all things considered, Maddie is lucky to be alive. She'll always have issues with her heart, but for the most part she'll lead a normal life."

"Now what? She's still too sick to go home, even if she has one."

"There's a children's center in Plano that specializes in the disorder. She'll be moved there until she's well enough to go home. And even then she'll need special care. She's still a very sick little girl, but at least now there's a light at the end of the tunnel. We have effective treatment options."

It was usually a happy occasion when a patient left the hospital, and while Clare was relieved that Maddie—that name would take some getting used to—was improving, she would miss the baby terribly.

"When are they moving her? I'd like to see her before she goes."

"She's being taken over by ambulance tomorrow morning," he said.

Clare fought the irrational urge to cry. "I want to get over there and spend some time with her."

"Of course. And I know this is difficult because we're all very attached to her. But it's for the best."

Logically, yes.

"Would you mind if I just lie here on the couch and take a catnap?"

"It will have to be a short one," Clare told Parker. "I won't be long."

"Take your time," he said with a huge yawn, putting his head back and closing his eyes. "I'm beat."

He looked beat, and kind of harmless. But she was still a little unsure…

"You're staying right here?" she said.

He looked up at her with bloodshot, sleepy eyes. "I'm not going to move, I promise. And this time I really do promise."

"I'll only be five minutes," she said.

His eyes slipped closed again and he mumbled something incoherent.

Feeling a little on edge, but also fairly certain he was telling the truth, she jogged upstairs to her bedroom. If she gave him too much time alone he might get bored and into trouble.

She picked her clothes out and laid them on the bed then went into the bathroom to brush her teeth and hair. She'd slept like hell last night. Not even a date with the water jets in her spa tub had been enough to soothe the restless, itchy feeling in her soul. She knew of only one person who could throw her into such turmoil, and he was napping on her couch.

She brushed the knots from her waist-length hair, reminding herself that it was time for a trim. She reached for a hair band, still thinking about Parker, wondering what he could be getting into down there. Her hand stopped in midair halfway to the drawer, then fell to her side, and she asked her reflection, "What *could* he be getting into?"

That was a really good question, because knowing Parker the way she did, he was definitely getting into some sort of trouble. He couldn't seem to help himself.

She frowned at her reflection. What the hell was she doing? Instead of making him promise not to snoop, she should have sent him on his way instead. Politely but firmly. It wasn't as if she needed him to drive her to the hospital. She had her aunt's car for that. He literally had no reason to be there. Other than to frustrate and annoy her.

Still in her robe she headed back down the stairs, calling out to her uninvited guest. "Hey, Parker, I was thinking—"

Parker didn't hear her. He was stretched out on her couch, hands tucked behind his head, sound asleep and snoring softly. He was taking a catnap, just as he'd said he would. But that wasn't what had her tripping over her own feet, or whimpering like a wounded animal.

Parker still had his pants on, which was a really good thing. Unfortunately that was *all* he had on. His shirt, undershirt, shoes and socks were on the floor beside the sofa. And oh, did he look good. Better than she had ever imagined he would.

Damn him!

Hard as she'd tried to deny it, there was definitely some sort of connection there. An irrational and scary kind of connection. It didn't make any sense. But lately it seemed that very few things in her life made much sense anymore. So if she just crawled up there with him…

You cannot let that happen, Clare.

No, she could not.

She closed her eyes and shook her head, wishing away the mental picture of him lying there looking all sexy and perfect. Wishing *him* away. But when she peeked through the small slit between her mostly closed lids he was still lying there, still looking amazing with his muscular chest and wide shoulders. And his abs? They were freaking perfect. She could do a million crunches a day and never look that good.

On the bright side, this was without a doubt the least obnoxious she had ever seen him. But now more than ever he really needed to go. And she really needed to stop staring at his chest.

"Parker," she said, keeping a safe distance between them. When he didn't respond she said it louder. "Parker!"

Still nothing.

She clapped her hands hard and loud, thinking it would startle him awake. He didn't even flinch.

This was not working.

She stepped just close enough to the couch so that she could reach him with her foot. She gave him a firm jab in the leg with her toes then stepped back. Parker kept on snoring.

Wow, he was out.

She stepped a little closer and nudged him again, then once more.

Nothing.

This was getting ridiculous.

She laid her foot on his stomach, intending to give him a good hard shake, right up until the second the sensitive bottom of her bare foot touched his warm, smooth skin.

Oh, that was dumb.

He didn't budge, and she realized, as she dropped her leg, that if he had woken he would have opened his eyes to an X-rated, full view of her goods from the waist down.

And why was she more disappointed than relieved that he remained asleep?

Okay, it was time to get serious. He really had to go. She wasn't thinking straight at all.

Using her opposite foot, in case he actually did wake up at some point, she hauled off and kicked his leg.

He mumbled something and shifted onto his side, facing her, and when he did his phone slipped out of his pocket, hit the hardwood floor with a thud and slid under the couch.

Crap.

She would have just left it there, but Parker was on call. If his phone rang he needed to be able to hear it.

Realizing that the odds of him waking at this point were slim to none, she got down on her knees and fished his phone out from under the couch, finding a couple of dust bunnies under there, as well.

Sitting back on her haunches she laid the phone on the arm of the couch next to his ear, then changed her mind and set it down on the cushion next to him. As she did, the backs of her fingers "accidentally" brushed against his stomach. She felt the contact with the intensity of an electric shock and it left her feeling limp and shaky.

This was getting out of hand fast, and she knew she should stop. Problem was, she really, *really* wanted to touch his abs. Not for long. She just wanted to know how it would feel. A few seconds tops. He would never have to know.

The idea of touching him was terrifying. And intoxicating. Her hands shook in anticipation. But did she have the guts to do it?

Her aunt was always telling Clare that she needed more excitement. That she was in the prime of her life, and she needed to take chances every now and then. Kay's life had been one long adventure, and despite what the family may have believed, she had no regrets.

Clare gnawed on her lip, fists balled tight. Should she or shouldn't she? He was sleeping like the dead. So what was the harm? It would quench her curiosity, and he would never have to know about it.

Just do it, Clare.

Her hand trembled as she reached out. She let it hover over his stomach for a second, so close she could feel the heat of his skin, working up the courage to take it one step further.

She was really going to do this. She was going to *touch* him.

Nervous, and excited, she lowered her hand, and the charge she felt as her skin touched his would have buckled her knees if she hadn't already been on the floor. The contrast of her pale skin against his much darker olive complexion was a crazy kind of erotic, and she sat there like that, watching his face for any sign that he was waking. She was playing with fire and it was more exhilarating than she could have ever imagined. It had been so long since she allowed herself to let go and follow her heart, she had forgotten how good it could feel to want someone. And now that she had a small taste of what it felt like to touch him, to be so close to him, she didn't want to stop.

Once she rang that bell, it was impossible to un-ring it.

She let her hand drift upward, toward his pecs, which were as impressive, or even more impressive, than his abs.

She looked back up at his face and froze. His eyes were open.

Damn, caught in the act. She muttered a very unladylike word.

"Am I dreaming?" he asked, his voice gravelly, eyes glossy from sleep, or lack thereof.

This had to be a dream. Real life never felt this good.

"You're dreaming," she told him, sliding her hand upward, through the sprinkling of silky hair on his chest.

He groaned and closed his eyes again. "If this is a dream I don't ever want to wake up."

"It is," she said, gently dragging her nails down his pecs, over his small dark nipples. The scent of his skin was inebriating, and so delicious she wanted to eat him up. "This isn't really happening."

A sleepy smile curled his lips. "So I can do this?"

He covered her hand with his own and lifted it to his lips, brushing a kiss against her wrist.

She whimpered and cupped his face in her hand, his beard rough against her palm. She brushed her thumb over his full bottom lip and his tongue darted out for a taste. It just about did her in.

"Come here," he said. He hooked his hands behind her neck and pulled her against the hard wall of his chest for a kiss. He tasted like coffee and sleep and something wild and exciting. Her heart pounded its way up into her throat and her skin felt electric. She was no longer thinking of the consequences. Screw the consequences. She wanted him, and she was going to take what she wanted.

His hand slid down her throat and slipped inside the opening of her robe, and when he cupped her breast, she stopped thinking altogether.

Seven

Her lips still pressed to Parker's, Clare climbed on the couch with him, straddling his thighs, her eyes dark with desire. He'd been fantasizing about this for so long, it was almost hard to believe it was really happening. When he first woke up to find her touching him, he thought it really *was* a dream. But if she wanted to pretend this wasn't happening who was he to shatter her illusion? If that was what it took to ease her conscience, to keep her in his arms, that was fine by him.

Then she was out of his arms, but only so she would be free to attack the zipper on his pants. She did it with the enthusiasm of someone on a time clock. Or someone trying not to change her mind. If she backed out now, the pain of what he would be missing out on would be excruciating. But it was a risk he was willing to take.

"No one can know about this," she said breathlessly

as she stripped him from the waist down. "And I mean no one."

Even if he wanted to disagree, there was no way in hell he would risk blowing this. Not now. He'd slept with a fair amount of women over the years. Sometimes the sex was fantastic, sometimes not, but they had all been missing something. The emotional connection he felt with Clare, maybe. He had never been one to chase women. The truth was he'd never had to. They always seemed to come to him. Maybe having to work for it made him appreciate the end result that much more. Because, damn, did he appreciate her right now.

"I promise I won't say a word to anyone." He tugged at the tie on her robe until it fell open. Clare whimpered softly. Either she believed him or she didn't care anymore.

"You're not worried about your aunt coming home?" he asked her.

"She's away for the week. She's always out of town."

"Good to know." Sliding his hands inside her robe, he pushed it off her slender shoulders, running his hands down her toned arms, over her soft stomach. She was all pale skin and soft curves, and everything in his being sighed with pleasure. She was perfect. Her dark blond hair hung like spun silk over her shoulders, giving him a peekaboo view of her perfectly shaped, supple breasts.

"You're amazing," he said. "I've never seen you with your hair down."

"Was it everything you hoped it would be?" She smiled at him with heavy-lidded eyes. "Because flattery will get you *everywhere*."

That was what he liked to hear.

"Will it get me here?" he asked her, cupping her firm

breasts, testing their weight against his palms, rolling the small pink tips between his fingers.

"Oh, yeah," she said, covering his hands with her own, showing him what she liked.

"How about here?" He ran his hands up her thighs, using his thumbs to tease the crevice where her legs met. She gasped as he touched her most sensitive spot. She was hot and wet and ready for him, but he wasn't about to rush this.

Clare had different ideas. She came up on her knees, and with one quick downward thrust he was inside of her. It was so erotic, and so unexpected, he nearly lost it right then. He moaned and his body arched upward to meet her, driving himself as deep as he could go.

Clare hissed with pleasure and threw her head back, her long hair brushing across his knees like the tickle of a feather. He gripped her hips, tried to slow her down as she rode him, but she was so deep in the zone, she didn't even seem to realize he was there.

Mild-mannered Nurse Clare had a naughty side after all.

She used his body, putting a friction shine on the leather sofa cushion, and he let her. When he was sure he couldn't take any more he wrapped his hands around her waist and tried to think about baseball, but she took him by the wrists and held them on either side of his head, using her weight to pin them there.

He could have easily gotten free, but why the hell would he want to? She seemed to get off on being in control, and he preferred a shameless and aggressive woman who knew what she liked. She could dominate him whenever and wherever she wanted.

Clare started to moan and ride him faster, and the

last shred of his control took a vacation. He never let himself be the first to orgasm, but he beat her to the punch by about thirty seconds. Clare didn't even seem to notice. She rode out her own release, then collapsed on his chest, breathing hard, her heart pounding in time with his own, and said, "I *really* needed that."

"Me, too," he said, folding his arms around her. Damn, she felt good. Holding her close this way was almost as good as the actual sex.

Almost.

He'd been anticipating this since the moment he'd first seen her, and she didn't disappoint.

She tucked her face into the crook of his neck, her silky hair catching on his chin stubble. "If I had known it would be this amazing I would have jumped you months ago."

"If I had any energy left, I would pin you down on the floor and do it again." He was so relaxed and so completely satisfied that he could barely keep his eyes open. Besides that catnap, which he was guessing by his intense fatigue couldn't have been more than a few minutes, he hadn't slept in more than twenty-four hours. As a resident he could function on one or two hours of sleep a night for a week or more, but he was getting too damned old now.

"Sure you won't change your mind?" she said, nibbling his earlobe.

Oh, man, did he want to. Maybe if he were ten years younger… "I wouldn't be much good to you like this."

She frowned, looking disappointed.

"I don't mean to sound ungrateful, because believe me, I'm not, but I have to know, why now?"

She shrugged. "I thought I would give the water jets in my tub a break."

Oh, damn. "Seriously?"

She grinned. "I shudder to imagine my next water bill."

The mental picture had his neurons firing and his blood boiling, but exhaustion won out. So he shelved the image for future reference. Not that he believed her. Or maybe he did.

"So," she said, disentangling herself from his arms to sit up, "I want to make sure we're on the same page."

Oh, boy, here we go. The Talk. "What? No afterglow?"

"I don't do afterglow. This isn't a relationship. This was just sex."

He'd used that same line on dozens of women and the irony of the situation wasn't lost on him. Because this time, he didn't want "just sex." He wanted her, in every way there was to want someone. It felt almost as if the force of the universe was propelling them toward one another. He knew that she felt it, too. She just wasn't ready to let herself accept it. But she would in her own time, and thankfully he was a very patient man.

"Whatever you want," he told her, and she looked as if maybe she didn't believe him.

"No one can know about us. And I mean *no one*."

"Be careful, you're going to bruise my tender ego."

She laughed and climbed off his lap, grabbing her robe from the floor. "Somehow I doubt that."

"Where are you going?"

"I have to get dressed and get out of here. I'd like to spend some time with Janey before they take her."

"Maddie," he reminded her.

"Right. It's going to be weird calling her by a different name. I also promised I would work a few hours at the free clinic this afternoon."

"Can I see you later?"

She hesitated, then said, "That's probably not a good idea."

"Why?"

She shot him a look as she tugged the robe back on. "You know why."

"I knew it," he said, throwing his arm dramatically over his eyes. "You're ashamed of me."

She grabbed his shirt off the floor and tossed it to him. "I need you dressed and ready to go by the time I come back down."

"Sure thing," he said, but the second she was gone he tossed his shirt on the floor and dropped his head back against the arm of the sofa. He must have drifted off, only to be roused by a loud thud.

He peered out through the slits of his eyes, trying to get his bearings, then saw his clothes in a pile on the floor beside the couch and grinned. Clare must have decided to let him stay, or maybe she had tried to wake him and he hadn't responded. The house was quiet and the angle of the sunshine filtering through the closed blinds meant it had to be late afternoon. Clare had covered him with one of her quilts before she left, and it smelled like her. He knew he should get dressed and get home for a few more hours of shut-eye, but he was so comfortable...

He looked back over at his clothes and a few feet away sat an unfamiliar pair of shoes. Women's shoes. He didn't recall them being there that morning. Clare hadn't been wearing them. Then one of the shoes started tapping, and he realized that there was an actual person inside of them.

And he had the sinking feeling that it wasn't Clare.

Parker bolted up on the couch, catching the blanket just before it fell to the floor.

The shoes were on an older, attractive woman, and the noise that roused him must have been the front door closing after she'd come in.

He was assuming she was Clare's aunt. So much for her being out of town.

Having heard her referred to as an old maid, Parker had formed a specific impression in his head of how Kay probably looked, but reality bore no resemblance to his imagination. Her clothes were casual but neat, fashionable and very expensive. She had long dark blond hair like Clare's, but hers was peppered with shades of silver and gray, and while Clare's hair had a sort of wild and free quality to it, this woman's was smooth and sleek.

Thankfully, she wasn't holding a gun on him. Because people in Texas loved their guns. And he was guessing she had one or two herself.

"It's not every day a woman comes home to find a naked man on her couch," she said with a heavy Texas twang. "This must be my lucky day." Then she looked him up and down, smiled and added, "Or maybe it's yours."

Boy did he hope she was joking. "You must be Aunt Kay."

"I must be."

He could only imagine what she was probably thinking, and damn would he like to put some clothes on. The blanket was feeling awfully thin and a little small.

"And who might you be?" she asked.

"Parker," he said. "Parker Reese. I work with Clare."

One brow rose slightly. "Among other things?"

No, this wasn't awkward at all. "Uh…yeah."

"You're better looking than I imagined. But that might just be the absence of clothes."

So she knew who he was? That was interesting. "Has Clare mentioned me?"

She gave him one of those *bless your heart* looks. "I'm afraid that I'm not at liberty to say."

Ooookay.

"She was right about one thing," Kay said. "They would have a field day with you."

Huh? "They who? And why would they have a field day?"

She flashed him another placating smile. "I'm not at liberty to say."

Of course she wasn't. This was too weird. He was the naked stranger in her house, yet he was the one asking all of the questions. Though she seemed to have a pretty good idea of who he was. "Maybe I should call Clare," he said.

"Maybe you should put your clothes on first."

Yeah, that would probably be a good idea. He just hoped she wasn't expecting to watch him.

"Go on up to Clare's room, and for the love of all that is holy, take the blanket with you. My heart isn't what it used to be."

Somehow he doubted that. Despite her age, she looked strong as an ox. Sturdy, yet refined. And as much as he appreciated the offer of privacy—and oh, did he appreciate it—he wasn't so sure Clare would appreciate him using her bedroom. He'd gone up there the other night to tease her, but this was different. It felt like an invasion of privacy to be in there when she wasn't around. If he was going to make this relationship work, he had to respect Clare's boundaries. "Would it be all right if I just use a bathroom down here? I don't want to invade Clare's space."

His request seemed to surprise Kay, and he was betting it earned him a few brownie points, too.

"That's awfully thoughtful of you. There's a half bath just off the kitchen."

"Thanks." He grabbed his clothes and his phone and with the blanket tucked firmly around his midsection, he hightailed it to the bathroom. Once he was in there, there was no hurry, but he threw his clothes on as quickly as possible. So fast he was pretty sure he put his boxers and socks on inside out.

When he was dressed he checked his phone, surprised to find that it was almost four o'clock. He'd slept for nearly *eight* hours. Far more than his typical five or six. And it was a deep restful kind of sleep that usually evaded him.

Must have been the sex.

He dialed Clare, and she answered her phone saying, "You had better not be snooping."

He smiled and shook his head. "Houston, we have a problem."

"What's wrong?"

"You know how you thought your aunt was still out of town?"

"Uh-oh."

Uh-oh was right. "Yeah, well, she's not. She's here."

He could feel her cringe over the phone line. "Tell me you weren't still on the couch."

"I wish I could."

"Naked?"

"As the day I was born."

She made a noise and it took a second for him to realize what he was hearing. "Oh, my God, are you *laughing*?"

"No, of course not," she said, clearing her throat. "She's not holding you at gunpoint, is she?"

He knew she had guns! "Not yet, and frankly, she's scary enough without one."

"Yeah, she can be," Clare said, and he could hear the mirth in her voice. Was she enjoying this?

"This isn't funny. Stop laughing."

"I'm sorry, but the mental picture…"

Okay, maybe it was a little funny. "I take it my name has come up before."

There was a slight pause, as if she were choosing her words carefully. "A time or two, yes."

"You don't seem too upset that our *secret* is out."

"Aunt Kay won't tell anyone. I trust her absolutely."

"She said that you were right, they would have a field day. What's that supposed to mean?"

"Long story," she said. "And I'm sorry she walked in on you like that. I really had no idea she would be home early."

"Are you coming back?"

"Not for another hour or so. I'm volunteering at the free clinic."

"So basically I'm on my own?"

"Yeah, sorry."

"You promise she's not going to hurt me?"

"If it makes you feel better, she's never actually shot anyone."

Oh, yeah, that made him feel so much better.

"However…" she said.

"What?"

"She might give you a hard time."

"*Might?* She already did!"

"Well, it's probably not over yet. Aunt Kay is very protective of me."

Swell.

"Did you see Ja—I mean Maddie?" he asked her. "I didn't get a page so I'm assuming things are good."

"I did see her, and she's doing really well. Logan and Hadley were there with Maggie. She's so much bigger and healthier, it's hard to imagine that they're the same age."

"Maddie will catch up."

"I'm going to miss her, but I know this is for the best. And I'm so glad to know that she has family."

"Did Logan say if he was able to contact his brother?"

"They left messages for him but so far they haven't heard back. Won't he be surprised to find out that not only is he a father, but to twins no less."

"And one with special needs. He'll have his hands full."

"Hold on a sec," Clare said, and he heard her talking to someone, then she was back. "Parker, I have to go. Can I call you later?"

He was hoping she would. "Of course."

"Okay, I'll talk to you then. And, Parker?"

"Yeah?"

"Good luck."

She seemed to be enjoying this a little too much.

He hung up and stuck his phone in his pocket, then folded the blanket he'd been wearing and opened the door. Clare's aunt was standing in the kitchen, sipping on a bottle of beer. She gestured to an open bottle in front of a bar stool at the kitchen island and said, "Have a seat, Parker."

"I should really get going," he said.

One brow rose slightly, and she gave him a look that said compliance was not optional.

Wow. She was tough. And a little scary.

No, she was *a lot* scary.

He handed her the blanket and did as he was told, feeling like a teenager meeting his girlfriend's parents for the first time. "I guess I can spare a few minutes."

"What are your intentions with my niece?"

Talk about getting right to the point. But who knew, maybe he would glean some insight on what made Clare tick. "I find her utterly fascinating," he said. "From the minute we were introduced I was drawn to her, and though she won't admit it, I think the feeling is mutual."

Kay neither confirmed nor denied it. "Clare is not as tough as she likes people to think."

"I know."

"She's a little broken."

"Who isn't?"

His answer seemed to satisfy her. "You're a smart man, but I'll be keeping my eye on you."

No surprise there, and he couldn't help but respect her for it. "Aunt Kay," he said, "I would expect no less."

Eight

It was just starting to get dark when Clare pulled in the driveway. Parker's car was gone, and she realized that deep down she had been hoping he was still there. Which was completely ridiculous. He had better things to do than hang around all day waiting for her.

But it would have been a little cool if he had. And a little terrifying.

She parked her aunt's car in the garage and stepped inside the house. "I'm home!"

"In here!" her aunt called from the living room.

Aunt Kay sat in her recliner, a book in her lap. She loved murder mysteries and psychological thrillers. The darker and gorier the better.

"So," Clare said, setting her purse down on the coffee table. "Is he buried in the backyard in a shallow grave?"

"Oh, please," her aunt scoffed. "There are much more effective ways to get rid of a body. And a car."

Clare gave her a look.

"I'm kidding. I like him."

Huh? Aunt Kay never "liked" anyone without getting to know them first, and that process could take weeks, and sometimes even months. "Just like that? You like him."

She shrugged. "Sometimes you just know. I would think you of all people would realize that."

"What's that supposed to mean?"

"You know *exactly* what I mean, Clare. You've got it bad for the man."

Yeah, she did. "He doesn't know that."

"He sure thinks he does."

Of course he did. He was a man. He thought he knew everything. It just so happened that in this case he was right.

Lucky guess.

"He is a little stubborn. I almost ran him to death on the jogging path the other day. Then I served him a half-frozen breakfast sandwich, which he actually ate. I should have known he would be too damned polite to complain."

"Sounds as if you've been having fun with him," Kay said.

"At his expense."

"Nothing wrong with that. Is he good in bed?"

Clare collapsed onto the sofa. "We never made it to the bed, but he's good on a couch."

"I'm just happy to hear that you're letting your hair down and having fun for a change. You need a man in your life."

"Don't get ahead of yourself." It had *bad idea* written all over it. She couldn't think straight when she was around him. All she could feel was an edgy sort of excitement, and she had been displaying a dangerously blasé attitude. She'd left him alone in her house, for God's sake. She *never* did that.

Although to be fair, removing him would have required dragging him sound asleep out the front door and leaving him on the porch. She'd tried to wake him when she was ready to go, but the man slept like the dead. "I haven't even decided if I'm going to sleep with him again," she told her aunt.

"Well, that just breaks my heart," Aunt Kay said. "A body that perfect should be put to good use."

Though she and Kay looked a little bit alike, and they both shared a deep aversion to farm life, Clare and her aunt couldn't have been more different. Kay grabbed life by the horns and didn't let go, while Clare wouldn't even venture on the other side of the fence.

"Here's something you might find interesting," Kay said. "I told him he could go up to your room to change."

Clare's jaw fell. "Why? You know I hate that."

"He apparently knows, too, because he asked to change in the bathroom down here instead. Said he didn't want to invade your space."

She blinked. "Oh."

"Sounds like he knows you pretty well already."

Yeah, it sort of did.

"And he respects your space."

Finally.

"And he's so hot."

Yes, he was.

"Maybe you should cut the guy a break and give him a chance. Not all men are liars and cheats. Something tells me that he's one of the good guys. Go out on a date or two. Have some fun, see where it goes."

"Why would I date someone that I can't even take home to my family? You said it yourself. They would have a field day with him."

"Maybe you should stop worrying about what they think."

She wished it were that easy. "How badly did you scare him?"

She shrugged. "If he scared easily you would have been rid of him months ago."

That still didn't make a relationship a good idea. It just meant that he was stubborn.

"I wish you could have seen the look on his face when he woke up and saw me standing there," Kay said with a smile. "If only I'd had my camera."

Clare would have paid big money to see that. "I hope you don't mind but I had to use your car. Mine committed suicide last night. It will cost almost as much as a new one to fix it."

"Of course I don't mind. Do we need to go car shopping?"

"I'm thinking it's time." Her aunt was a ruthless haggler. Be it a car or a refrigerator, when the salesman gave his rock-bottom price, she always managed to talk him down just a little lower. When they were rebuilding the house after the tornado she'd haggled the builder into paying out of pocket for the upgrades the insurance refused to cover. People just had a hard time telling her no.

"What brought you home so early?" Clare asked her.

"Claud and I had a fight. He asked me to marry him again."

"I take it you said no?"

She sighed, shaking her head. "Some men never learn."

She could have been talking about Parker, but Clare didn't bother to point that out.

"Are you hungry?" Kay asked. "Let's order dinner."

"I could go for sushi."

"Hmm, sounds good," she said, pulling out her phone. Neither of them cooked, so her aunt had the number of every restaurant in Royal that delivered on speed dial. "You want the usual?"

"Yes, please. While I'm waiting I'm going to go upstairs and get out of these scrubs." She was exhausted, thanks to a certain someone waking her at the crack of dawn that morning. But in all fairness it had been worth it.

"I'll let you know when it gets here," her aunt told her.

With sore, tired feet Clare climbed the stairs. A soak in the tub sounded good, but with the food on the way she took a hot shower instead. And though they were barely stubbly, she shaved her legs and cleaned up the bikini line, as well.

Just in case.

After her shower, as she was drying off, she took note of her new svelte figure. She looked damn good. Not that she'd been overweight, per se, but she hadn't exactly been healthy before.

She was still standing at the mirror naked, brushing the knots from her wet hair when her aunt knocked on the bedroom door. "Come on in! Just leave it on the bed."

She heard the door open, then close again, and a second later saw movement in the bathroom doorway. She turned and her breath caught in her lungs.

It was Parker standing there.

He grinned, his eyes raking over her from the top of her head all the way down to her pink-tipped toes, and every inch of her skin came alive all at once. He looked sexy as hell in faded jeans and a black T-shirt with the hospital logo. She had never seen him dressed so casually. She took in the way those biceps stretched the armholes of his shirt, and the way the jeans hugged his lean hips. But as good as he looked in his clothes, she knew he looked even better out of them.

He held up the sushi bag and said with a frustratingly sexy smile, "Special delivery."

Clare would have grabbed her robe to cover herself, but by the look in his eyes, and the fact that he had put the bag down and begun to peel off his clothes, she had the feeling the damage was already done.

"Your aunt sent me up," he said, taking off his shirt and dropping it on the floor. "Remind me to thank her profusely."

Aunt Kay would hear about it later, all right. Because she was meddling. Unfortunately she was really good at it.

The jeans went next, and Clare just stood there like a dummy watching, when she should have been kicking him to the curb for being so presumptuous. But then the boxers dropped and that was all she wrote. She couldn't tell him no now if her life depended on it.

"Come here," he said, taking her hand and leading her to the bed, walking backward so he didn't have to take his eyes off her. "You are so sexy."

Before she could censor herself, she said, "Look who's talking."

With a grin, he pulled her in and kissed her. And

kissed her. Oh, did she love kissing him. He smelled freshly showered and his chin was smooth. And as he hauled her up against the length of that ripped physique she was no more sturdy than her trembling hands. Lucky for her he wasted no time getting her off her feet and into bed.

He laid her on her back. Typically she didn't like being on her back, but as he climbed in beside her, she decided to let it slide. Then he started to kiss her again and she ignored that irrational need to be in control. She liked the feel of his weight pressing her into the mattress, his hands skimming her body, igniting a trail of fire across her skin. Then he began to kiss his way downward. It felt so good, and she wanted to relax and enjoy it, but as he reached the lowest part of her stomach, she automatically tensed.

Parker froze and lifted his head to look at her. "What's wrong?"

"Nothing."

He frowned and pushed himself up on his elbows. "Don't lie to me."

Damn it. Why did he have to be so intuitive? So concerned about her needs and her weird hang-ups. He needed to stop being so wonderfully thoughtful. "It's nothing."

"The hell it is. Talk to me, Clare."

The tone in his voice when he said her name sent shivers across her skin. After months of listening to the annoying nicknames he came up with for her, he had to choose *now* to start using her real name? When she was feeling most vulnerable? And did he have to say it with so much...*feeling*?

"What you're doing, what you're getting ready to do, it makes me feel very…"

"Vulnerable?"

"*Yes*. Very vulnerable."

"Do you want me to stop?"

"Yes. And no. I don't know, it's weird. I'm weird."

To his credit he didn't ask why she felt that way, because that was one big ole can of worms she would rather not spill just yet. Or maybe ever. He was just so darned open and honest, it was difficult not to give him some sort of explanation.

"You're not weird." He kissed her stomach once more, then made his way back upward. "And I don't want to do anything that makes you uncomfortable. This is supposed to be fun."

"I don't want you to think that I don't trust you."

"Clare, you barely know me. Trust is earned." He kissed her so sweetly she could have cried, or punched him, then he rolled onto his back and pulled her on top of him, grinning that devilish smile. "Better?"

"You don't mind?"

"I get to lie here while a gorgeous woman rides me like I'm a rodeo bull. What do you think?"

She leaned down to kiss him, for fear that if she didn't do something, she really would cry. Why did he have to be so wonderful? So understanding?

So damn *hot*.

He clearly had no reservations about being dominated, because she did ride him like a rodeo bull. He let her take the lead and set the pace, and even though he was on his back he didn't just lie there. He kept his hands and his mouth and his hips plenty busy making her crazy, and when he cradled her face in his hands and gasped her name as he shattered, that sent her sailing. Her own release came on like a tsunami that set her soaring headlong into ecstasy.

And he wasn't even through with her. He rolled her over and started from the top again. Her senses blurred and her body quaked and she forgot all about being in control, being nervous, and let him do his thing. And boy, did he do his thing. When she couldn't take it any longer, he was still champing at the bit to pleasure her again.

She'd rediscovered muscles tonight that she hadn't used in a long time, and it was way past time to take them out, dust them off and put them to good use. But she was going to pay for it tomorrow.

"I need to rest," she told him, flopping down on her back.

"I've heard that more than once tonight," he said with a grin, his hand teasing its way downward.

She intercepted it just above her navel. "I really mean it this time. I'm exhausted."

Looking disappointed, he rolled onto his back beside her. She didn't usually do the afterglow part, but as he took her hand, weaving their fingers together, she was too tired to move. Besides, it felt good to be near to him, their bodies close, their fingers intertwined. She liked it way too much.

"So what did my aunt say to you when you got here?" she asked him.

"She handed me the bag and said, 'Clare is in her bedroom, go on up.'"

She and Aunt Kay were going to have to have a talk about boundaries. About how it was not okay to send sexy men up to her bedroom. Although in this particular case Clare was willing to overlook the transgression.

"Your aunt is tough," he said. "But I think she likes me."

She wouldn't have sent him up here otherwise. "She has to be tough. She's been on her own most of her life. At a time when women didn't stay single and have careers instead of families."

He pushed himself up on his elbow. "She's never been married?"

"She was once, a really long time ago. But only for a few months."

"What happened? If you don't mind my asking."

"As a kid Kay hated farm life. Probably more than I do. She always dreamed of being a 'sophisticated city slicker,' as she put it. When she was seventeen she met a wealthy businessman from Tulsa. He was fifteen years older and worldly and she fell hard for him. Everyone loved him. He was charming and personable, and he showered her and her family with gifts. He took her to fancy restaurants and bought her nice clothes.

"I guess times were pretty hard and her parents were so happy to have a rich son-in-law, they didn't bat an eyelash when she turned up pregnant. So they had a shotgun wedding, then he took her to his house in Tulsa. Everyone thought he was perfect, and that Kay was such a lucky girl."

"No one is perfect."

"Yeah. They were married about a week when he started beating her."

Parker winced. "He was a predator."

"A predator with a volatile temper. She said he was like Jekyll and Hyde. The first time he hit her it was over the grocery money. He got angry because she bought a magazine. She called him stingy, and he back-handed her."

Parker cringed. "She didn't leave?"

"She had nowhere to go. Her parents were too poor to take her and her baby in, and back then a pregnant woman couldn't just go out and get a job, or even get a credit card without her husband's signature. Plus, he'd been subsidizing her family's farm. She knew that if she tried to leave, he would cut them off. Without that money, they would have fallen into poverty and lost everything. There would be no place for her parents and her five siblings to go. She was, as she puts it, in one hell of a pickle."

"Did her parents know what was going on?"

"No, of course not. If they had they would have driven to Tulsa and taken her back home, even if it meant losing everything. But she said the guilt would have hurt far worse than his fists ever could."

"That's one hell of a sacrifice. But she obviously got away."

"Yes, when he almost killed her. He came home from work angry and she said the wrong thing, so he used her as a punching bag. It was dumb luck that a neighbor had her window open and just happened to hear him screaming at her. When he stormed off the neighbor came by to see if she was okay. She found her bleeding and battered on the kitchen floor and called for help. Kay had internal injuries and would have bled to death if not for her. They got her to the hospital in time to save her life, but she lost the baby. And her uterus."

He closed his eyes and shook his head. Jesus.

"But she made sure it would never happen again. To her or anyone else."

"How?"

"Long story short, the day she got out of the hospital he said he was going to teach her a lesson, so she ran him over with his car."

His eyes went wide and his jaw fell. "Did she kill him?"

"Almost. He never walked right again. Or beat anyone else, I'm sure."

"Did she get in trouble?"

"She claimed it was self-defense, and after the way he beat her before that, people believed her. And Kay being Kay, she pulled herself up by her bootstraps and started over. When she was healed she wound up getting a job as a stewardess. She worked the international flights, so she's traveled pretty much everywhere, and has friends all over the world. When she was labeled 'too old' to do the job, she started a travel agency in Dallas. When the industry was at an all-time high she retired and sold the business for a small fortune. Now she spends most of her time traveling and volunteering for domestic-abuse organizations. She counsels young people trapped in abusive relationships."

"Wow, that's one hell of a life."

"I keep telling her that she needs to write a memoir. Her story could help a lot of people."

Parker's stomach rumbled loudly and Clare laughed. "Hungry?"

"I guess I skipped dinner," he said, rubbing a hand across his belly.

"I've got sushi and I'd be willing to share. And I could probably find a couple of beers in the fridge."

For several seconds he just looked at her, a funny little half smile on his face.

"What?"

"You surprise me, Clare."

"Why is that?"

"I thought for sure you would kick me out of your bed the second we were finished."

So did she. And normally she would have. "If I wasn't so tired I probably would," she lied, when the truth was she didn't want him to go anywhere.

She was playing a dangerous game, letting him get so close. If she wasn't careful she might do something stupid like fall head over heels in love with him.

Nine

Though she'd had only one day off work, when Clare pulled into the hospital lot the next morning it felt as if weeks had passed. So much had happened in such a short span of time.

She and Parker had had a picnic on her bed last night—sushi and beer—then had sex again. She couldn't imagine where he found the energy. He had impressive stamina, and loads of patience. She must have fallen asleep immediately afterward, and when she woke at midnight he was gone. He could have easily taken advantage of her unconscious state and hung around, but he really seemed to respect her space now. As hard as he'd pushed the past three months, suddenly he seemed to know just when to back off. It was a little disconcerting—no, make that terrifying—the way he was so attuned to her needs. Most men didn't have a clue.

Parker was in meetings all morning so she didn't see him right away, and as a result spent the first half of her day fighting the nervous excitement building in her belly. It wasn't as if she didn't see him almost every day at work. What a difference a few days could make. It felt as if her entire life had been flipped on its head. And somewhere in the back of her mind there was a nagging little voice asking her, what if it was all a game to him? What if he said something to make people believe they were an item. What if he hauled her up out of her chair behind the nurses' station and kissed her senseless?

As quickly as she had the thought, she dismissed it. Now that she knew him a little better, she didn't think he would be capable of anything so underhanded. Her aunt was right: he was one of the good guys. And Clare needed to get her priorities straight.

In her experience, the hotter the sex, the faster the relationship burned, until there was nothing left but ash. At the rate they were going, they wouldn't make it a week.

But he had been so sweet and so understanding about her reservations. Because of her hang-ups, a first intimate encounter with a man could be a bit awkward, and usually was. Men always thought they would be the one to "cure" her. As if she was broken or something. Which she was a little, she supposed. But they inevitably pushed her too far, or sometimes not far enough. It just always seemed to end in disaster for everyone. Eventually, she'd just stopped trying.

But this thing with Parker had her reevaluating that decision.

She was at the nurses' station looking up a chart on the computer when she heard his familiar footsteps, and as he neared, her heart sailed right up into her already tight throat and lodged there, pounding relentlessly.

Oh, man, this was *bad*.

She heard him talking to Rebecca. Clare knew for a fact that he'd dated the young nurse a time or two, and Clare felt her hackles rise. Though from the look on Rebecca's face when Clare glanced up, there was no love lost there. Her eyes settled on Parker for no more than a second, but the damage was done. Her heart did a nosedive with a triple twist to the pit of her belly, knocking her insides all out of whack.

She heard him send Rebecca to check on a patient, then his footsteps as he came closer. Her heart sailed back up into her throat again and the crown of her scalp felt tingly and warm.

"Hey there, sweet cheeks," he said, which was exactly the way he would have greeted her before they slept together. And it would have annoyed the hell out of her. Now the sound of his voice strummed across her nerve endings, the friction warming her from the inside out.

"Dr. Reese," she said, not looking up from the screen. She was afraid that if she looked at him again, her true feelings would wind up on display for everyone to see. Including him. She was so beside herself her hands were trembling.

What was *wrong* with her?

He leaned down and looked over her shoulder at the computer screen, as if they were discussing a patient, and said quietly, "Have I mentioned that you're amazing?"

It was difficult not to swoon, or throw her arms

around his neck and kiss him. Hoping her voice wasn't as shaky as the rest of her, she said, "Once or twice."

"Sleep well?"

She nodded. Oh, had she ever. He had completely worn her out. "I was a little surprised that you left."

"You sound disappointed."

Yeah, she sort of did, didn't she?

"I would have stayed." He pointed at nothing in particular on the screen. "But I left because I knew that would be what you wanted."

And he was right. Or was he? If she had woken up beside him this morning, they could have had a little fun before work.

Which just goes to show how much this is clouding your judgment, you big dummy.

He really needed to get a handle on this habit he had of being so wonderful. Couldn't he say something sexist or rude? Or even better, condescending.

"Busy tonight?" he asked.

"What were you thinking?"

His breath was warm against her ear when he said, "You know exactly what I'm thinking, cupcake."

Back to the nicknames, were they? She was sort of getting used to hearing him use her name. But this time the teasing didn't bother her so much. "I promised my friend Violet that I would go to a stained-glass class with her tonight at Priceless, the antiques store just outside of town."

"Sounds like fun. Violet is Mac McCallum's sister, right? He owns the Double M Ranch."

"That's the one."

"Okay," he said. "How about afterward?"

She wanted to, she really did. It was all just moving

so fast. "I think I need some time to think. You know, about us."

"At least you're willing to admit there is an *us*."

At least.

As he straightened, his hand brushed her bare arm and her senses went into extreme overload. "Call me if you change your mind, princess."

Clare really, *really* wanted to see him tonight, and wrestled all day with what she should do. Should she be smart and reasonable, and take the time she needed to sort her feelings out, or be wildly irresponsible, say what the hell and jump him again? When Violet called later that afternoon to confirm their plans, Clare felt torn.

After small talk about the ranch she and her brother Mac owned, Violet asked, "Are we still on for tonight?"

An excuse was on the tip of her tongue, and Clare would have canceled, but the idea of seeing Parker socially four days in a row scared her a little.

"I can't wait," she told Violet with more enthusiasm than she was feeling. But she also knew she was doing the right thing. She was sure when she got to Priceless she would have a good time. She'd always had an interest in making stained glass and she'd heard that Raina Patterson's studio was impressive. In addition to teaching crafts, Raina sold antiques out of the space. Clare had shopped in Priceless, but never taken a class there.

She remembered her car situation and asked Violet, "I know it's a little out of your way, but could you give me a lift? I'm carless right now."

"Is that how you wound up at the Royal Diner with

Dr. Reese the other night?" Violet asked, a teasing lilt in her tone.

Ugh. Clare hated small towns sometimes. Violet was well aware of Parker's shenanigans and how much they irritated Clare. She and everyone else Clare knew.

She made a sound of disgust and said, "He basically kidnapped me. He offered to drive me home then took me to the diner instead. Short of walking, or calling a cab, I was stuck. But I was hungry and he paid the check, so it could have been worse, I guess."

"Why don't you just go out with him?"

"Because he's a womanizing, insufferable, megalomaniac."

"Yeah, but he's *so* hot."

"Then why don't you go out with him?"

There was a slight pause, then she said, "It's not me he wants."

Touché.

She heard footsteps behind her and turned to see Grace Haines, Janey's caseworker, approaching. *Madeline*, she reminded herself. For a second she thought the worst, that something was wrong, but Grace was smiling.

"I have to let you go, Violet. I'll see you tonight."

They hung up and Clare greeted Grace with a smile and a hug. "What brings you here?"

"I came to pick up some paperwork for Madeline's transfer and I thought I would stop and say hello."

"How is she doing?"

"She's great. She may get to go home in a couple of weeks. She'll have monitors, of course, but Hadley and Logan are taking a class at the center so they'll know what to do in an emergency."

"No word on the father?" Clare asked.

Grace shook her head somberly. "Either he can't be reached, or doesn't want to be. Logan doesn't speak too highly of his brother. Thankfully if Seth doesn't claim the twins, Logan and Hadley have already committed to adopting them. Honestly, I'm thinking that it would be for the best. I'm all for keeping children with their biological parents, but Seth is anything but reliable."

"After such a rotten start in life, those girls deserve a happy, stable family."

"They sure do," Grace said. "I dated Seth in high school. Even then there was nothing *stable* about him."

"Grace!"

Clare and Grace both turned to see Parker coming toward them, all smiles. "How's my favorite caseworker?"

Grace smiled. "Great, and how is my favorite pediatrician?"

"Couldn't be better," he said, not even acknowledging that Clare was standing there. Then they hugged and though it was totally platonic Clare felt the slightest twinge of jealousy. Grace was tall and curvy with chestnut hair that tumbled down in soft natural curls. She was also beautiful, and so very nice, and Clare had never met a caseworker more dedicated to the kids in her care. Standing together she and Parker made an extremely attractive couple.

"How's our girl doing?" Parker asked her.

"Still improving. I was just telling Clare that she might be able to go home in a couple of weeks."

"That makes my day," he said.

Grace looked at her watch. "I'd love to stay and chat but I have a home visit to get to. But I'm sure I'll see you guys again soon."

"It was great to see you," Parker said, then he turned to Clare and his smile disappeared. "When you get a minute I need to see you in my office."

Her heart plummeted and landed with a messy splat. He looked genuinely upset with her and she had no clue what she had done wrong.

"Um, yeah, sure," she said. "Now is good."

He nodded sternly, turned and all but marched down the hall. The two women watched him walk away in stunned silence.

"What was that about?" Grace asked, looking as taken aback by his demeanor as Clare was.

"I have no idea. I guess I'm about to find out."

"Well, good luck."

They headed in opposite directions down the hall. When Clare got to Parker's office the door was partially closed so she knocked gingerly.

"Enter."

She stepped inside expecting to see him at his desk. Then the door shut behind her and she spun around. Parker stood there grinning. "Hey there, sweet cheeks."

"Hey," Clare said, looking hopelessly confused.

Parker took her hand and pulled her against him, then proceeded to kiss her socks off. When he finally let her go she gave him a playful shove. "You creep! I really thought you were mad at me."

"Pretty good, huh?" Parker said with a grin. He probably could have made his point without sounding angry, but the crushed look on Clare's face had been worth it. If he'd snapped at her a week ago, she would have stood there stony faced and emotionless, as if she only had to listen because he was the boss. Not that he snapped at his staff all that often, but it did happen occasionally. But her reaction said something that up until now he could only hypothesize.

She cared. A lot.

She slid her arms up around his neck, pressed her body to his and pulled him down for an enthusiastic kiss. He got an instant hard-on. She was sexy as hell, and so completely unaware of it.

"Did you really need to talk to me or did you just want to make out?" she asked him. "Because the longer I'm in here the more suspicious it will look."

"I saw the way you looked at us when I hugged Grace. I thought we should talk about it."

"How did I look?" she asked, even though she knew that he knew exactly what was going on.

"A little green, actually."

She backed out of his arms, nose in the air. "That's ridiculous."

"Is it?"

She folded her arms stubbornly. "Yes, it is."

"Admit it, you were jealous."

"Why would I be jealous? We're not in an exclusive relationship."

"Well then, maybe we should be."

Her eyes went wide and up went the wall. "That's crazy. I haven't even decided if I'm going to sleep with you again."

Yeah, right. "Then what was that kiss you just laid on me all about? Are you a tease, Clare?"

She didn't seem to have a comeback for that, but her inner struggle was written all over her face.

"You do what you need to do," he told her. "But as

long as we're *involved*, I'm not going to date, or have any sort of physical relationship with anyone else."

She looked as if she might cry, or barf. As if she didn't know *how* to feel. And all she managed was a shaky, "O-okay."

He tugged her back into his arms with no resistance and tipped her chin up so he could look into her eyes. "That's a promise, sweetheart."

Something dark flashed in her eyes. "In my experience men have a very limited grasp on the concept of a promise."

"Sounds like you've been hanging around the wrong kind of men."

Clearly he'd hit a sore spot. She untangled herself from his arms and said, "This is not the time or the place to get into this. I have to get back to work. If anyone asks, we're discussing Janey—I mean, Madeline's case. Finishing up paperwork or something."

He nodded. "As you wish."

After she left, he took a seat at his desk. Boy, had he hit a nerve.

Luc popped his head in a second later. "Hey, have you got a minute?"

"Sure, what's up?"

He flopped down in the chair opposite Parker and propped his feet up on the desk. "I haven't seen you in a few days so I wasn't able to congratulate you on solving the mystery."

Mystery? Had he somehow figured out that Parker and Clare were intimate?

He decided to play dumb. "I'm not sure what you mean."

Luc looked at him as if he was an idiot. "Madeline. I hear that she's getting better."

Oh, *that mystery.* "Twin-to-twin transfusion," he said with a shrug. "Who knew?"

"Was that Clare I just saw leaving your office?"

"We were discussing a patient," he said.

"I also heard you were at the diner with her the other night. Sounds as if you're wearing her down."

It took a second for Parker to realize that Luc was referring to their bet. Parker had completely forgotten about it. What seemed like an innocent joke then could have real repercussions for his relationship with Clare if she ever caught wind of it.

"Actually I haven't made any progress at all. And I'm thinking I'm just wasting my time."

"You might want to rethink that," Luc said. "I mentioned our bet to Bruce Marsh in Radiology and he wanted in. He must have told someone, and they must have told someone else. Last night I heard a member mention it at the club."

Suddenly Parker was the one who felt like barfing. And he couldn't even get angry because it wasn't unusual for their little bets to make the rounds of their fellow doctors. To have this one running rampant through the hospital was bad enough. Now that it was out in public, God only knew who would get wind of it.

What the hell had he done?

"I'm clearly not getting anywhere with her, so let's just call you the winner and be done with it," he told Luc.

Luc frowned. "It's not like you to give up so easily. Is there something you're not telling me?"

He wrestled with his options. If he told Luc the truth

he would be breaking a promise to Clare, but if he didn't he could find himself in the hot seat.

Breaking a promise to Clare to save himself? Really? That sounded like something his father would do. There had to be a better way.

"The truth is, I've started seeing someone," he told Luc, sticking as close to the truth as possible. "She works here at the hospital and wants to keep the relationship quiet while we see where this goes."

His curiosity piqued, Luc asked, "Is it someone I know?"

"Maybe. Maybe not. But I have strong feelings for this woman, and if she hears about the bet she might take it the wrong way."

"I see what you mean," Luc said. "I'm sorry, Parker. I'll see what I can do to make this discreetly go away, but it seems to have taken on a life of its own."

Parker felt sick to his stomach. How the hell had he gotten himself in this mess? What had he been thinking? Innocent bet or not it had been sexist and chauvinistic. That was exactly the person he'd been struggling *not* to be. There was a time when he saw women as playthings…as an interesting and pleasurable way to pass the time. And while he'd never been openly or deliberately disrespectful to any member of the opposite sex, his actions spoke for themselves.

If Luc couldn't get a handle on this, Parker would have no choice but to fess up to Clare and take his lumps. Even if that meant losing her.

Ten

As promised Violet picked Clare up on the way to Priceless.

It was currently housed in a giant renovated red barn in the Courtyard, the growing artist's community on the outskirts of town. Clare used to be a regular shopper in the antiques store when it was located downtown, but it had been devastated by the tornado. Since Raina had changed locations, Clare never seemed to get out that way often enough. Seeing all of the amazing stock up front in the shop as Raina led them back to the workshop was motivating Clare to come back very soon.

Violet had been quiet for most of the drive there, which was very unusual for her. She was one of the spunkiest women Clare knew. And weirdly enough, Clare, who was usually the quiet type, couldn't seem to stop talking. She felt all bubbly and excited inside, while at the same time questioning her own sanity.

Exclusive, my ass. How could the hospital playboy make such an outrageous claim? She was betting that he'd never even been in a committed relationship. Now he wanted one with *her*? They didn't even...*match*. He should be with someone like Grace. Someone as beautiful as he was.

Once they were inside the building under the bright studio lights, Clare realized that Violet didn't look so good. Her skin looked especially pale against her thick auburn hair, and Clare could swear she was a little thinner than the last time she saw her.

When the class was under way, she leaned close to Violet. "Are you feeling okay? You look a little green."

The minute the words were out she realized that Parker had said nearly the exact same thing to her earlier today. Oh, great, he was beginning to rub off on her.

"I don't know what's wrong," Violet said, sipping gingerly on the water bottle she'd brought to class. "I'll be fine for a while, then get this weird overwhelming nausea. It must be some sort of virus."

It didn't sound like a virus to Clare. "When do you seem to feel sick the most?"

"I wake up feeling pretty lousy every day, and though I'm starving all the time, if I eat I can barely hold it down. I've been really tired, too."

Clare made her voice even lower and asked, "Is there any possibility that you're pregnant?"

Violet sucked in a breath and a myriad of emotions flashed across her face. Shock, fear, confusion. Then she shook her head and said, "No, that can't be it. I'm not even seeing anyone."

"Are you sure, because early prenatal care—"

"That's not it," she insisted. "It's just a virus or a parasite or something. I'll be fine."

Clare let it go, but a few minutes later, as she snapped a piece of glass in the wrong place, Violet nudged her with her elbow and whispered, "Oh, my God! Is that a hickey?"

Clare glanced at the people sitting around them. "Where?"

"On your neck, genius."

Clare gasped and slapped a hand across the side of her neck, felt herself starting to flush. "No, of course not."

Violet wasn't buying it. "You haven't stopped smiling since I picked you up and you practically talked my head off on the way here. No wonder you've been in such a good mood."

She was going to deny it. Say that it was… Well, that was the problem. She didn't know what to say. Besides, the inferno burning in her cheeks was a dead giveaway.

Violet leaned in close and whispered, "Did you do what I think you did? And if so, with whom?"

Clare opened her mouth but nothing came out.

"Was it Dr. Reese?"

Still speechless, Clare just looked at her, and Violet's eyes went wide. "Oh, my God, it *was* him!"

"Shhhh," Clare scolded, as people turned to look at them. "Keep your voice down."

"I knew it," Violet whispered. "I knew you had a thing for him. And who can blame you?"

"You can't tell anyone," Clare said, tugging the band from her hair so it would tumble down and cover the evidence. "And I mean *no one*."

"Why? You guys make an adorable couple."

No, he made her look good. He and Grace? *They* made an adorable couple.

"I'm not even sure if I'm going to see him again," she told Violet. "If people knew it would just be awkward. You have to promise me you won't say anything to anyone."

"Of course I promise," Violet said, laying a reassuring hand on her arm. "But you can't keep it a secret forever."

If she tried hard enough she could. The alternative was unacceptable. If her staff were to learn how flighty and irresponsible she'd been behaving, they would lose all respect for her.

Parker still on her mind, Clare could hardly concentrate on the class. And no matter how hard she tried she couldn't get the damned glass pieces cut without mangling them horribly.

First stained-glass class. Major fail.

She looked up and saw Raina's little boy Justin, dressed in a cowboy get-up, clomping around the perimeter of the room as if he was riding a horse.

Their eyes met and Clare waved. Justin changed direction and trotted over to her table.

"Hey there, partner," Clare teased, then realized almost immediately that she sounded just like Parker and his silly nicknames. He really was starting rub off on her.

But Justin giggled and stopped at her table, all smiles. "Hi, Clare."

"I like the threads," she told him, tugging on his fringed faux-suede vest.

"Santa brought it," he said, very matter-of-factly. "*And* he brought me a *daddy.*"

Clare gasped. *"No way!"* Everyone knew that Raina and Nolan Dane were engaged, but Clare played along, telling Justin, "You must have been super good all year."

"Super, *super* good," he said proudly.

"Hey, mister," Raina said to her son, stopping at the table to check Clare and Violet's progress. "Do we bother the customers during classes?"

His little bottom lip rolled into a pout and he shook his head.

"Skedaddle."

He sighed and said, *"Okay."*

Raina chucked him on the chin and he trotted off on his invisible steed. Then she looked down at the mess on Clare's table and tried to smile.

"I guess stained glass just isn't my thing," Clare told her.

"It takes practice," Raina said.

Not to mention concentration and a steady hand. Neither of which Clare possessed at the moment. She still couldn't believe Parker had given her a hickey, when he knew how important it was to keep their relationship secret. If people in town got wind that she was seeing someone—*anyone*—she would be under the microscope. Because that's the way it was in Royal. Everyone was all up in each other's private business.

The longer she thought about what he'd done, the angrier she became, and by the time Violet dropped her at home she was so hot under the collar it was a wonder steam wasn't shooting out her ears. She knew she had to settle this or she would be up all night fuming.

Thankfully her aunt was home. She sat in her recliner reading one of her murder mysteries.

"Would it be okay if I use your car?" Clare asked her.

"Sure, hon, help yourself." Her head tipped a little to the left. "Are you okay? You look upset."

Upset didn't begin to say it. "You have no idea."

"Uh-oh. Parker?"

"I'll explain when I get back." She dialed Parker's number on her way to the garage.

"Hello," he answered.

"I need your address."

There was a slight pause. "You do?"

She started the car and initialized the navigation. "Yes, I do."

He recited the address and she punched it in. He was only fifteen minutes away. "Thanks."

"You don't sound happy."

"I'm not."

"So why did you want my address?"

"So I can come over there and kill you."

Parker wasn't sure what was going on, or why Clare would be unhappy, but it didn't take long to find out. She got there in ten minutes flat and started pounding on his front door. He opened it and there she stood on his porch looking *incredibly* unhappy. After they'd hung up he'd wondered if this was some sort of revenge for pretending to be mad at her earlier that day.

Apparently not.

"Whatever you're unhappy about, I'm certain it's not the door's fault."

She glared at him. "You gave me a *hickey*?"

Was that what had gotten her panties in such a twist? He stepped back and gestured her inside. "Come on in. Let's talk."

She charged past him. "Violet saw it, and she made me admit I'm seeing someone. And she knows it's *you*."

"Clare, I didn't give you a hickey."

She made a rude noise. "Well, I didn't give it to *myself*."

"Let me see," he said.

She took her coat off and dropped it over the back of the couch, baring her neck to him. "See? How do you explain that?"

He examined her neck. "Explain what?"

"What do you mean, what? Don't tell me you don't know what a hickey looks like."

"Clare, there's nothing here."

Her lips pressed into a tight line. "That's not funny."

"I'm not trying to be funny. Is it maybe on the other side?" Frowning, she turned so he could look. "Sorry, nothing there either."

"How can that be? Violet said—" She blinked, then blinked again. "Oh, my gosh, that little sneak."

"I don't get it," he said.

She collapsed onto the couch, dropping her head in her hands. "She suspected that I was seeing someone so she lied about the hickey to make me spill my guts. And I fell for it, hook, line and sinker."

Was that all?

"I'm sorry," she said.

"It's okay." He sat down beside her, took her hand, which she promptly retracted.

"No, it's not. I'm an intelligent person. You'd think that I would have the good sense to at least confirm it in a mirror before I started flinging accusations."

"I could think of a few ways you could make it up to

me," he said, but he didn't get the smile he'd been hoping for. He wasn't sure if she'd even heard him.

"This is ridiculous," she said, and was up on her feet again, pacing the rug. "I'm acting like a crazy person."

He took her hand to hold her still. "Don't you think you might be overreacting a little? I'm assuming you told Violet the truth because you trust her." Or because deep down, she actually wanted the truth to come out. It was too soon to say.

She looked up at him. "Did you mean what you said today? About being exclusive? It wasn't just a line to get me back into bed?"

They were back to that? He should have known that this wouldn't be easy, that she would question his every move. What had made her so afraid to follow her heart?

"Come here," he said, pulling her down into his lap, surprised when she didn't resist. He looked her dead in the eyes, so she would know he was telling the truth, and said, "It was not a line. I meant every word I said."

She looked as though she really wanted to believe him but wasn't quite there yet. Which was a little frustrating, but not a deal breaker. She would get there.

"Have you ever even been in a committed relationship?" she asked him.

He shook his head. "Nope."

"Then how can you promise to be exclusive to me? Do you even know how?" She paused then said, "Don't answer that."

Oooookay.

She looked around his living room, as if actually seeing it for the first time since she got there. "Nice condo. Although I would have imagined you in something a lot bigger. I like the decor, though."

"It's an executive rental—it came this way."

"Oh."

"I'll buy something eventually. I just thought I should settle into the job first, before I tied myself here."

"So you're not sure you're staying?"

Definitely not what he'd said. "I wasn't sure *then*." He picked up her hand and kissed the inside of her wrist. "But I am now."

"If you tell me you're staying because of me, I'll probably have a panic attack. Just sayin'."

He grinned. "No panic attacks tonight."

"I'm sorry."

"Would you *stop* apologizing?" He rearranged her on his lap so she was straddling his thighs. "I have a great idea. Why don't you kiss me."

"You're just trying to shut me up."

He grinned. "Pretty much."

She tried to look offended, but laughed instead. "There is such a thing as *too* honest, you know. But this time, I guess I'll let it slide."

"I think it's time for a tour of the house," he told her. "Specifically my bedroom, though I do have a fairly sturdy desk in my office. Just sayin'. Or there's the trundle bed in the spare room—"

She folded a hand over his mouth, a saucy grin on her glossy lips. "We can do it wherever you want. Now, shut up and kiss me."

Despite all the options Parker had mentioned, they went to the bedroom first, then never left. Every time she told herself that the sex couldn't possibly get better, he pulled out the stops, making her even crazier than he had the time before. It was as if someone had written a handbook on her emotional and sexual needs, and he'd read it from cover to cover. Twice.

Afterward he pulled on a pair of flannel pajama bottoms and headed to the kitchen for a snack. Which wound up being leftover reheated spinach and bacon quiche— coincidentally, her favorite kind—and a huge bowl of grapes. And it was delicious. They sat side by side on his bed, eating the quiche and feeding each other grapes.

"This is so good," she said, and always on the lookout for palatable frozen fare, asked, "What brand is it?"

"It's not," he said.

"Oh. Did you get it from a restaurant?"

He looked at her a little funny. "No."

"Does someone cook for you?"

He shook his head. "Guess again."

"Elves?"

He laughed. "Is it really so hard to believe that a man can cook?"

In her family it was. "The men in my family don't cook."

"How about you?"

"I was banned from the kitchen a long time ago. Forget to turn off the burner under the frying pan and almost burn down the kitchen *one time*, and you're branded for life." Which was fine because she had always hated cooking. And still did. "You really made this?" she asked.

"I really did." He popped a green grape in her mouth. She bit down and the sweet juice exploded onto her tongue. Lately food seemed to taste so much better than before. In fact, everything about her life felt pretty darn good.

If only she could let go and just trust it. Trust him.

YOUR PARTICIPATION IS REQUESTED!

Dear Reader,

Since you are a lover of our books – we would like to get to know you!

Inside you will find a short Reader's Survey. Sharing your answers with us will help our editorial staff understand who you are and what activities you enjoy.

To thank you for your participation, we would like to send you 2 books and 2 gifts – **ABSOLUTELY FREE!**

Enjoy your gifts with our appreciation,

Pam Powers

**SEE INSIDE
FOR READER'S
SURVEY**

For Your Reading Pleasure...

We'll send you 2 books and 2 gifts
ABSOLUTELY FREE
just for completing our Reader's Survey!

YOUR READER'S SURVEY
"THANK YOU" FREE GIFTS INCLUDE:
- ▶ **2 FREE books**
- ▶ **2 lovely surprise gifts**

PLEASE FILL IN THE CIRCLES COMPLETELY TO RESPOND

1) What type of fiction books do you enjoy reading? (Check all that apply)
○ Suspense/Thrillers ○ Action/Adventure ○ Modern-day Romances
○ Historical Romance ○ Humour ○ Paranormal Romance

2) What attracted you most to the last fiction book you purchased on impulse?
○ The Title ○ The Cover ○ The Author ○ The Story

3) What is usually the greatest influencer when you _plan_ to buy a book?
○ Advertising ○ Referral ○ Book Review

4) How often do you access the internet?
○ Daily ○ Weekly ○ Monthly ○ Rarely or never.

5) How many NEW paperback fiction novels have you purchased in the past 3 months?
○ 0 - 2 ○ 3 - 6 ○ 7 or more

YES! I have completed the Reader's Survey. Please send me the 2 FREE books and 2 FREE gifts (gifts are worth about $10) for which I qualify. I understand that I am under no obligation to purchase any books, as explained on the back of this card.

225 HDL GJ2D/326 HDL GJ2E

FIRST NAME

LAST NAME

ADDRESS

APT.#

CITY

STATE/PROV.

ZIP/POSTAL CODE

D-216-SUR16

◀ If offer card is missing write to: Reader Service, P.O. Box 1867, Buffalo, NY 14240-1867 or visit www.ReaderService.com ▶

BUSINESS REPLY MAIL
FIRST-CLASS MAIL   PERMIT NO. 717   BUFFALO, NY

POSTAGE WILL BE PAID BY ADDRESSEE

READER SERVICE
PO BOX 1867
BUFFALO NY 14240-9952

NO POSTAGE
NECESSARY
IF MAILED
IN THE
UNITED STATES

"Can you cook anything else?" she asked him.

"Anything you want, as long as I have the ingredients. And a recipe."

"Did you take classes?"

"I dated a chef. We saw each other on and off for about six months, I guess. She would cook for me and I would watch. Then I started experimenting on my own. I realized I was pretty good at it, and I found it incredibly relaxing. And I'm not gonna lie, the chicks dig it."

"Hit me again," she said, nodding to the grapes.

"For someone so trim you sure can put the food away." He fed her another grape, the pad of his thumb grazing her lower lip.

"I've lost almost twenty pounds since December."

He looked genuinely surprised. "Seriously?"

"Seriously."

"That's a lot."

"Did you not notice that I was a bit on the chubby side?"

He shrugged. "You looked good to me. Besides, chubby is okay."

Was this guy for real? "Aside from your weird fascination with me, I was under the impression that you were more attracted to the Barbie-doll type."

"So was I."

What the hell was that supposed to mean? Was he deliberately trying to confuse her?

"So what changed?" she asked him.

"I saw you."

If it was a lie, it was the sweetest lie anyone had ever told her. And the idea that it might be true scared her half to death. "Haul out the boots and shovels," she said. "The BS is getting deep."

He laughed. "Why is it so unbelievable?"

"Because everyone knows the kind of man you are. You're a womanizer and a serial dater. That sort of guy doesn't settle down. He conquers. And when he gets bored he moves on. And even if he does eventually settle, it never lasts."

"Yep, that pretty much sounds like me."

She blinked, taken aback by his honesty. He sure wasn't helping his case. "So I'm right?"

"I didn't say that."

"What *are* you saying?"

"People change. Priorities change. I'm not the man I used to be."

In her experience, people could change, but not that much. "So you're telling me that you're ready to settle down?"

"I don't know. Maybe. There was a time when I never would have considered a wife and kids. Now it doesn't seem so far-fetched."

He would make an excellent husband and father, and she envied the woman who snagged him. And she wished that it could be her. Even though she knew it was impossible.

"As much as you love kids, I'm surprised you don't have any," he told her. "Just haven't found the right man?"

She hadn't even been looking. "My patients are my children," she said. "Besides, I'm only thirty-three. I still have a few good childbearing years ahead of me. Or maybe I'll follow in my aunt Kay's footsteps and never have any. God knows there are enough of us already. Another baby in the family would be like white noise. Especially a child of mine."

Eleven

"Why is that?" Parker asked Clare.

"Forget it," she said with a shake of her head, as if she were clearing away an unpleasant memory. "It's a long story."

Something told him not to push the issue of her family, but eventually they were going to talk about it, and he was going to get to the root of the problem. Even if he had to take drastic measures. The key to her heart was in there somewhere under all the baggage, and he was going to find it.

But for now he would let it slide.

"By the way, I noticed last night that the toilet in your bathroom was running like crazy," he said.

"I know. I have to call a plumber."

"You want me to take a look at it?"

"You know how to fix a toilet?"

"Yup."

"What kind of millionaire are you?"

He laughed. "Not a very good one, I guess."

"You sure don't act like a rich guy."

"Are you forgetting? I drive a luxury import."

"That you put a Santa hat and antlers on for Christmas."

He grinned. "I like Christmas."

"And you are the least pretentious person I know. There's a rumor going around that you give a lot of your money to charity."

"My *dad's* money," he said. "And my reasons are not as philanthropic as you might think. I give his money away to charity because I know that's the last thing he would want me to do with it."

"Not the charitable type?"

"For him it was all about making more money. It was never enough. He died a very wealthy man, but his money never did anyone much good. Not even him."

"And now it does."

"Exactly. I may have to live with the millionaire label, but that doesn't mean I have to like it."

"So, when did you learn to fix a toilet?"

"My father believed I should know everything about running his business, from the ground up. Including building maintenance. So instead of letting me volunteer for Greenpeace during summer break—which is what I really wanted to do—I was forced to follow George the maintenance guy around for three months. I thought it was all a total waste of time. As a doctor I wouldn't need to know how to fix a toilet or unclog a drain."

"Unless your home toilet breaks and the plumber can't make it over for a week."

"Exactly. Looking back, I'm thankful for everything I learned. I really have used a lot of that knowledge in my adult life. Not everything he taught me was a total waste of time. His tyrannical way of running his business taught me the best way not to talk to my staff. He thought that he was better than anyone who had less money than him. I was supposed to take over his business. Instead, I sold it all off before the body was cold."

Her brows rose.

"I know that sounds crass, and probably a little selfish, but the offer was made and I took it. I never wanted his business. From the time I was small I was into nature and conservation. There was a time when I seriously considered becoming a veterinarian."

"No way."

"I loved animals, and it got me into trouble sometimes."

"How so?"

"When I was a kid, maybe thirteen or fourteen, I got wind of a project my dad and his company would be working on. They were trying to buy land and develop on a nature preserve. I went on a campaign to stop them."

"You must have been a really confident kid to take on not only a huge company but also your own father."

"I'm not sure if it was confidence, stupidity or just a glaring lack of common sense, but when he figured out what I was up to he grounded me for a month."

"And you said that your mother wasn't around?"

"It was a pretty strange situation actually. My father

hired my mother as a surrogate. He wanted an heir, a mini me, if you will. Long story short, they fell in love."

"Wow, it sounds like the plot of a romance novel or movie. What could be more romantic?"

"Shortly after my birth she left us both for the limo driver."

Clare cringed. "Okay, so not that romantic," she said. "How sad that must have been for your father, especially with a newborn baby."

"I think he was more angry than sad. For pretty much my entire childhood he drilled into me that women were all liars and cheaters and were not to be trusted. He considered them playthings."

"And you believed him?"

"You hear something enough times, you can't help but believe it. He more or less had me brainwashed."

One bad experience and Parker's father felt the need to judge all women? "What a horrible thing to do to you," she said.

"I had money to burn, a career I loved and women champing at the bit, willing to do pretty much anything to land me. And I let them, knowing damn well I would never settle down. In my eyes, life should have been perfect. In reality I felt empty, and disgusted with myself. At that point I knew things had to change. I can't really blame my mother for leaving," Parker said. "If you knew my father you would understand why. To put it in simple terms, he was a bully. It was his way or the highway."

"So you've never even met her?"

He shook his head. "I haven't even seen a picture. I thought I might find some when he died, but he probably burned them."

"If she thought your father was that terrible, why did she leave you there with him?"

"I've asked myself that same thing a million times."

"I just… I don't understand. I'll *never* understand how a woman could leave her own child."

"I'll probably never know why she did it, but I'd like to think she left out of her love for me. That I was somehow better off without her. I guess I'll never know for sure."

"You've never tried to find her? It probably wouldn't be that difficult."

"I'm not difficult to find either."

There was so much buried pain and bitterness in those words it hurt her heart.

"Why don't we talk about something else?" he said, stretching out across the bed and pulling her down with him. "Or better yet, let's not talk at all."

Tempting, but there was something she had to say to him, something he deserved to hear, hard as it would be. She untangled herself from his arms and sat up. "No, we do need to talk."

He sat up, too. "What?"

"I need to explain to you why I'm the way I am. You know, my need to be in control of myself at all times. Especially in bed."

"Clare, you don't have to explain."

"No, I do. I want you to understand." She took his hand between her two and squeezed it. "I trust you."

The smile he flashed her made her feel all warm inside. She was starting to believe that he genuinely cared about her. Which was awful, of course, and wonderful. And she didn't have a clue what to do about it.

One step at a time, Clare.

"This happened a long time ago, at my first job out of nursing school. Before I started working at the hospital I worked very briefly at an OB-GYN practice. It was my first real job besides working on my parents' farm and I was incredibly naive. One of the doctors sort of took me under his wing. Then into his bed."

Parker looked pained, but stayed quiet.

"He was older, and way more sophisticated. I felt so honored that he picked me. For a month he was my entire world. We had to keep it a secret, of course. For my sake, he said. So it wouldn't look like favoritism. I thought we were falling in love, then his pregnant wife showed up at the office."

Parker mumbled a curse. "I take it you didn't know he was married?"

She shook her head. "He never talked about her, or even had a picture in his office. I didn't have a clue. Needless to say I ended it the second she was gone. I never would have gone near him if I knew. He came on strong and was so persistent."

"And I did the same damn thing, didn't I?" His laugh was a wry one. "All the time I thought I was being charming, you thought I was a total creep."

She cracked a smile. "Well, not a *total* creep."

"I'm really sorry, Clare."

"There's no way you could have known. Besides, I'm not the person now that I was back then. I'd been so sheltered up to that point. My family is really big and very traditional. My parents wouldn't even talk about letting me date until I was seventeen, and by then I was cramming to get on the honor list so I could get a scholarship and get the hell out of there. Nursing school was brutal, so I spent most of my time studying. I didn't have much experience with boys, and I had virtually no experience with men. It never even occurred to me that a married man would initiate an intimate relationship. Where I was from men didn't do that sort of thing. Or if they did, no one talked about it."

"So what happened? Did the pregnant wife find out?"

"She found an old text that he'd saved. A very personal and explicit text."

"You were sexting."

She nodded. "She was not happy about it. It was a huge blowout. He said that *I* seduced *him*. Needless to say I lost my job. And my dignity. No one believed me when I said I didn't know he was married."

"It wasn't your fault."

"Most people didn't see it that way, my family included. I was devastated and I needed someone to talk to. My aunt was away on business and I couldn't get ahold of her. I called my sister Sue instead. Growing up, she was the one I was closest to. I made her swear that she would take it to the grave. Two minutes after we hung up my mother called in hysterics. She said that I should have known better and I should come right back to the ranch where I belonged. I was a simple country girl and people would always try to take advantage of me. And it was high time I realized that I would never make it on my own, and I needed my family. She wouldn't even let me try to explain. She ended the conversation by saying how disappointed she was in me."

"That's a tough one," he said.

"It gets worse. My dad called me later that day to say that the family had had a meeting and everyone agreed that I had to come home."

His eyes went wide. "Your mom told the whole family?"

Clare nodded. "Of course I told my dad no, I wouldn't be coming home. I was too ashamed and mortified to show my face. No one even bothered to ask if I was okay. Then my siblings started calling me, trying to shame me into coming back home, saying how much everyone missed me. It's horrible when everyone you love and care about turns their back on you. I was devastated."

"You had every right to be. They betrayed your trust."

"They would tell you that I betrayed theirs."

"They're dead wrong. And shame on your brothers and sisters for not being there for you."

"Aunt Kay was the only one who believed me. Who cared. She invited me to come stay with her until I was back on my feet. I spent most of the first month in bed. But Kay was friends with the hospital administrator at Royal Memorial and she got me an interview. I didn't want to go, but she insisted. It was probably the best thing she could have done for me. With work to focus on I was able to put what happened behind me. Originally I had planned to get my own place, but we realized that it didn't make sense. Kay only uses the house as a home base when she isn't traveling, which isn't very often. She likes having someone here to keep an eye on things. It ended up being a perfect situation for both of us."

He shook his head, looking baffled. "I don't even know what to say."

"You don't have to say anything. Besides, I'm not finished."

"It gets worse?"

"I've only ever told Aunt Kay, because I knew she of all people would understand. It's very difficult to talk about the things that he did to me. But I have to tell you."

He looked pained. "You don't have to tell me."

She took a deep breath and blew it out, trembling from head to toe. "No, I want to. I *need* to."

He put his hand on her shoulder. "Only if you're ready."

"He was my first. And I know that sounds crazy considering my age, but I wanted to save myself for someone special. It's how I was raised. I honestly thought he was the one. That's why I let him do what he wanted to do."

"Which was?"

She swallowed hard. *You can do this.* "He liked it… rough."

Parker winced. "But not your first time. Right?"

Though she wanted to bow her head in shame, she held it high instead. "He didn't force me, and I could have said no, but I was so head over heels for him, I would have done anything he asked. Even though it terrified me. He got off on my fear."

Looking confused, Parker asked, "So, am I to understand that every time you had sex with him, you were scared? Or am I way off base?"

She took a deep breath and blew it out. "*Every* time. Some more than others. It depended on his mood. Near the end of the relationship he had begun to get very aggressive. And again, I could have walked away. I chose to stay."

"This doctor have a name?" Parker asked, jaw

clenched. "In honor of your dignity and self-respect, I'd like to kick his teeth in."

"He wouldn't be worth the effort. He was a sleaze-bag. He'll probably always be one. It was just poor judgment on my part."

"Listen to me," Parker said, gently cradling her face in his hands. "It's not your fault."

She folded her hands over his. "I know that now, but it still stings after all this time. I'm still humiliated. Without fail, every time I'm visiting the farm someone makes a snide remark about the relationship. They'll never let me live it down."

"You're giving them way too much power," he said.

"Probably. And I hope that someday I can let it go. I'm just not ready yet."

"What can I do?" he said.

"Just be patient with me. "

"I can do that," he said with a smile. After everything she'd just revealed, all the pain she had spilled out, she could smile, too. It felt good to talk about it. To let off some of the pressure.

"After it was over, it took years before I wanted to have sex again," she told him, "and a long time after that before I could let myself enjoy it. I've come a long way since then, but I'm still not one hundred percent there. Maybe I'll never be."

"No, you will be."

Twelve

Parker sounded so sure, Clare wanted to believe him. If anyone could pull her back from the dark recesses of her mind, it would probably be him. For whatever reason, he seemed to "get" her. And she was nowhere close to ready to admit that to him.

"I'm thirsty. You want something to drink?" she asked him. She needed a minute to regroup, and could see the understanding in his eyes.

"I could go for a beer," he said.

"I'll be right back." She hopped up from the bed and headed downstairs to the kitchen. It was a very nice condo, but as she got a better look around, it seemed a little barren and impersonal. Definitely temporary. She wondered what sort of place he would be looking for...

Nope, she didn't even want to know, because what if it was exactly the same thing she wanted? That would just be awkward.

The refrigerator was well stocked with a variety of foods. Lots of fruits and vegetables and cheeses. She grabbed two beers off the door and headed back up. After this beer she had to go home. She'd never done well sleeping in strange places. She was a creature of habit. If she stayed here, in an unfamiliar bed, she would probably toss and turn all night long.

Yeah, Clare, just keep telling yourself that.

The truth was that she was scared, plain and simple.

And wasn't she being a little presumptuous? He hadn't even asked if she wanted to stay. It was possible that he didn't even want her to.

As if. He would probably love it. It would make him very happy.

A cold chill raised the hair on her arms. Wasn't that exactly what had gotten her into trouble before?

Don't you want me to be happy? her ex would ask when something he did made her uncomfortable. *You know I would never do anything to hurt you.*

It was a lie. He wasn't happy *unless* he was hurting her.

But this was different. Parker went out of his way to make *her* happy. She thought that telling him the truth about her past would make her feel vulnerable and weak, but in reality she felt empowered. And it was a *good* feeling. She felt good when she was with him. So why was she still fighting this? Everything about their relationship felt right. He seemed like someone she could really learn to trust. She was already partway there. Didn't she owe it to herself to at least *try*?

When Clare stepped back into the bedroom Parker was sound asleep and snoring softly. And here she thought he'd worn her out, when it looked as if it was the other way around. She considered waking him, but he looked so adorable when he slept.

She set the beers down on the night table and slid into bed beside him. He was facing her, so she could lie there and watch his beautiful face all night if she wanted to.

She thought about his mother abandoning him and her heart broke. It was so sad she wanted to cry. No wonder he didn't let himself get close to women. The most important woman in his life had walked away without looking back. And his horrible father had only exacerbated the problem by filling his head with lies.

It made her wish things could be different for him, that she could be the one to make him see that mother or no mother, he was an amazing human being. Truly one of the good ones.

She must have dozed off, because when she opened her eyes again the lights were out and she was in the exact same position on the bed. Parker was gone.

She rubbed her eyes and rolled over to grab her phone, which was almost dead. Six o'clock.

She'd done it. She'd spent the night and the world hadn't come to an end. And she hadn't slept lousy either.

She leaned over and switched on the lamp, temporarily blinding herself. As her pupils adjusted, Parker walked into the room wearing his flannel pajama bottoms, holding two steaming cups of coffee.

"Good morning, sleepyhead," he said, his usual chipper, cheerful self. He may have been the most positive, upbeat person she had ever known.

She pushed herself up into a sitting position. "Good morning."

He handed her one of the cups, sat on the edge of the mattress beside her and kissed her forehead. There was something so sweet about it, so deeply affectionate. "Sleep well?"

Amazingly well. "I must have been in a coma," she said. "I didn't move once. I don't even think I dreamed."

"I did," he said, wiggling his brows, "but we'll save that for later."

Hmm, something to look forward to.

"Did you mean to stay, or did you fall asleep before you could leave?"

"A little of both."

"Are you sorry that you stayed?"

She smiled and shook her head. "But I can't stay long. I have to go home and get ready for work. And return my aunt's car."

"How are you planning to get to the hospital?"

"Kay can drive me."

"Or you can shower here. I'll follow you home, wait while you change, then take you to work."

And risk being seen together? That would most certainly get the rumor mill spinning.

She was getting sick of living afraid, always worried about what people would think of her. Maybe it was time she got her priorities straight. Maybe it should be about what she wanted for a change.

"Okay."

He looked a little taken aback, but he smiled. "Really?"

"Really. It's on your way. Why not."

"If you want I can drop you around the block, so no one sees us together."

She did and she didn't. And what did that say about her? She was acting as though he was some dark, dirty secret when really, their relationship was far from controversial. They were two consenting adults and what they did outside the hospital was no one else's business. As long as they didn't let the physical relationship bleed into their work relationship. She already lost one job that way.

"I have to stop worrying what other people think. Like you said, I give people too much power."

"True story," he said with a smile. "So, you want me to shower first? Or we could even shower together."

"One step at a time," she said. Though most people wouldn't consider something as innocuous as sharing a shower a "step," they probably hadn't been brutally shoved face-first into a shower stall and pinned against the cold, hard tile.

Parker accepted her decline with a smile, because that's who Parker was. "I'll go first."

Her eyes glued to his tight behind as he walked to the closet to pick out clothes, she felt around the bedside table for her phone so she could check the weather. The low battery warning flashed, then the screen went black.

Damn.

"Do you know what the temperature is supposed to be today?" she asked as Parker laid his clothes out on the bed. "My phone just died."

"Look it up on my phone," he said. He leaned over to grab it off the bedside table and held it out to her.

She hesitated.

"I promise it won't bite."

She took it. "You really don't mind me looking at your phone?"

"Why would I? The code is 0613, my birthday."

"You were born on the thirteenth of June?"

"And yes, it was a Friday. I looked it up."

Well, that explained a lot.

"To me a phone is a very personal thing," she said. "I would never give out my code. Practically my whole life is on this phone."

"Me, too. If you did feel the need to snoop, you would probably find something interesting. You might even see something you wished you hadn't. Or you could just not snoop. Your choice."

She looked at the phone, then back at him. "You have my word, I definitely won't snoop."

He laughed. "I'll be out in ten minutes."

The following week Clare got a surprise call from her sister Jen. "I'm going to be in the area this afternoon picking up a mare, and I want to come see you," she told Clare.

Clare cringed, thankful Jen couldn't see her through the phone. Every visit with a family member seemed to end in disaster, and things had been going so well lately, she hated to push her luck. The past week and a half had been weird but wonderful. Clare *felt* wonderful. All her family ever did was bring her down. "I'm working today," Clare told her sister.

"I know, but you can take a quick break, right?"

"I have patients to care for. I can't just leave them." It was a lie. She could have asked someone to cover for her.

"But we haven't seen you in months. I miss you."

Don't have anyone else to embarrass and shame? she wanted to ask. "I'm sorry. Maybe if you would have given me a little advance notice."

"I only found out this morning that I had to go."

"Oh."

"You can't spare five minutes to see your own sister?"

Clare could feel herself caving. It was the guilt that always got her. "Tell you what. Call me when you get to Kay's house and I'll let you know if I can get away."

"I'll call you in about an hour."

And Clare wouldn't answer the phone. Problem solved.

She stuck her phone in her pocket. Maybe she was being selfish, but she wanted to be happy just a little while longer before she opened that wound again. She was learning that it was okay to be selfish every once in a while.

She got a text and looked at her phone again. It was from Parker, asking to see her in his office. They were extremely careful to keep their relationship platonic and professional at the hospital, but every so often they would meet in his office to steal a kiss or two. Sometimes more. Once when they were both working late he summoned her to his office and she found him sitting behind his desk wearing nothing but his lab coat and stethoscope.

His door was closed when she got there, so she knocked.

"Come in."

He was fully dressed—darn it—and sitting at his desk, his laptop in front of him. "Come in and close the door."

"What's up?"

"I need your opinion on something." He turned the laptop around so she could see the screen. "I've been on this site. It's called Family Finder. They help people connect with their biological family."

"Are you thinking of contacting your mom?"

He took a breath and blew it out, brow furrowed. "Since we talked about her it's been on my mind. I was thinking about Maddie and Maggie. They'll never get the opportunity to meet their real mom. But I can meet mine, and I can't deny that I'm curious."

"I think it would be a great idea."

"All I need to do is fill out a form with the information I have, which thankfully is extensive. If she's already posted on the site looking for me, I'll be notified."

"So, if she's already on the site, you'll know it right away."

He nodded. "I'm not sure how I feel about that. On the one hand I feel as if it's time to deal with this, and on the other I can't help but worry that I'll be disappointed. The forms are all filled out and ready to go. I'm just having a little trouble hitting Submit."

She loved that he wasn't too macho to let her see his vulnerabilities. He was very honest about his feelings. Sometimes too honest, so much so that it made her squirm a little. He knew the *L* word was currently off the table, but that didn't stop him from creatively hinting around. But he did it with so much charm it was difficult to be annoyed.

"I don't know what to say."

He snapped his laptop shut. "I have to think about this."

"There's no rush."

He pushed himself up from his chair. "Sorry to drag you in here for nothing."

She rose up on her toes and kissed him. "No problem."

They both walked out to the nurses' station. She sat

down, ready to get back to work, and Parker asked, "Are you expecting company?"

How could he possibly know that? "Did you bug my phone or something?"

"No, but there's a woman who just stepped off the elevator and she looks like she could be your twin."

Oh, crap! Clare shot up in her chair, and sure as anything there stood her sister by the elevator. How had she gotten there so fast?

Jen saw Clare and waved.

Parker was looking at her, waiting for an explanation.

"It's my sister Jen," she said. "I asked her not to come, but that's my family. Constantly ignoring what I say."

"Hey, sweetie," Jen said, and Clare walked around the station to hug her.

"An hour away?"

"Okay, I lied. I was already in Royal when I called you. And I didn't come for a horse. I came to see you."

Thirteen

"Dr. Reese," Clare said, hoping he would play along. "This is my sister Jen."

"Pleasure," Parker said, shaking her hand.

"Dr. Reese is my boss," she told her sister, hoping she would be less likely to say something embarrassing or inappropriate. Of all her siblings, Jen, six years her senior, was the most vocal, and the most blunt.

"You must be proud of your sister," he said, "being chief nurse of one of the highest-rated children's wards in the state."

"We all are," Jen said, shooting Clare a look.

Somehow Clare found that very hard to believe. They had never supported her in her career.

"We would be lost without her." Parker laid a hand on Clare's shoulder, giving it a reassuring squeeze. Then he flashed one of those charming smiles. "If you'll excuse me, ladies, I have a patient to check on."

"That man is like a cool glass of lemonade on a hot day," Jen said.

My *cool glass of lemonade, thank-you-very-much.* "Last I checked you were a married woman."

Jen grinned. "It doesn't hurt to look, honey. As long as I bring my appetite home."

Clare grimaced. "Ew."

Her sister laughed. "Can we go somewhere private and talk?"

Alarm made her heart skip a beat. Was Jen here because something bad had happened? "Sure, we can use the break room."

"Sounds good."

She showed her sister down the hall to the break room, which thankfully was empty, and said, "Have a seat."

Jen made herself comfortable in a chair. "So, are you and the doctor…?"

Oh, boy, here we go. "What makes you think that?"

"He was a little defensive, and you didn't seem to like me lookin' at him. And he squeezed your shoulder. That was a little personal."

"You noticed all that?"

"Honey, I have four boys. I don't miss a thing."

Clare raised her chin a notch, ready to take her lumps. "As a matter of fact, we're dating."

Jen nodded approvingly. "He's cute."

Clare waited for more. For a rich-doctor crack. Or some other disparaging remark.

"Is it serious?" Jen asked.

"We've only been dating for two weeks."

"Beau proposed to me on our second date. Fifteen

years later and we're still going strong. I think if you know, you just know. You know?"

Clare laughed, remembering why, of all her siblings, Jen was by far the most honest and outgoing. "You're weird."

She smiled. "That's what my boys tell me."

Times like now, Clare missed being a part of her family, wished she wasn't such an outsider. "So, you said you needed to talk to me. About what?"

"The seven of us had a family meeting."

"Seven?"

"Just the siblings."

"About what?"

"You mostly, and the fact that you never come around. And when you do you're so defensive."

Confused, she asked, "What about Mom and Dad? Were they at this meeting?"

"They weren't included."

As far as Clare knew, the family never made a group decision without first getting their parents' blessing. "You had a family meeting without Mom and Dad?"

"It's been known to happen. It wouldn't surprise you if you came around, or called."

"I'm busy."

"You want to talk about busy, try being the mom of four rambunctious boys, and I still make it to dinner at Mom and Dad's once a month. If we at least knew why you're so distant..."

"*Why?* Are you kidding me?"

"I know that something happened between you and Mom and Dad. I know what a pain they can be, but you have a very large family who misses you."

A kernel of anger popped in Clare's belly, causing

a chain reaction, until she felt like exploding. She'd always hated confrontation, but right now she was too furious to think straight. To be afraid. The new Clare stood up for herself, and didn't take any crap from anyone, damn it. "You miss me? Well, where the hell were you all when I needed you? When my entire world fell apart. You didn't miss me so much then."

"Clare—"

"I'm not stupid, you know. I know what you all think of me. What Mom and Dad think of me. You've made it obvious that I'm a huge disappointment."

"Clare—"

"People make mistakes, you know, but they shouldn't have to pay for it forever! It wasn't even my fault!" she shrieked, and for the first time actually believed it. "I was young and stupid and he took advantage of me. He lied to me. End of story."

"Clare, shut up!" Jen shouted.

Startled, Clare closed her mouth.

"What the *hell* are you talking about?"

She was going to play dumb? Seriously? "I know Mom and Dad told everyone. They said there was a family meeting. She said that everyone agreed I should come home. I was a simple country girl who could never make it on her own."

"We all knew something was wrong," Jen said. "But there was no family meeting. If Mom and Dad said there was, they were lying. They told everyone that you were in trouble, but they refused to say how or why. They just wanted us all to call and try to get you to come home. We were all worried sick about you. We still are. We want you back in the family."

"If Sue had kept her mouth shut, no one would have

known anything. She promised me she would take it to her grave, then she turned around and told Mom."

Jen frowned. "No, she didn't."

"*Yes*, she did."

"No, Clare, she did not. She heard Mom on the phone with you and assumed you had called her."

"If she didn't tell her, how did Mom find out?"

"If I had to guess, I would say she was listening on the extension. She used to do it all the time."

Taken aback, Clare blinked and said, "Since when?"

"Since my entire childhood. That's how she kept tabs on all of us."

Clare had no idea. But she hadn't spent much time on the phone as a kid either. And if she did it was to discuss homework, or equally innocuous things. She hadn't had much of a social life.

"She did it to everyone?"

"Yup. She was always listening to our calls and going through our stuff. There was no privacy in that house."

And Clare had thought it was just she who had no privacy. Had it not occurred to her that her brothers and sisters felt the same way?

"Sue seriously didn't tell them?"

"No, Clare. She wouldn't tell *anyone*, and we badgered her, believe me. We wanted to know what was wrong. Anytime we tried to bring it up, you went on the defensive. Then you stopped coming around. We were all very hurt."

Clare could barely wrap her head around it. All these years she had stayed away, thinking everyone was judging her, and they didn't even know what had happened? "She really didn't tell anyone?"

"No, hon," Jen said patiently. "She didn't."

Tears stung Clare's eyes. Was it possible that what she had conceived as wisecracks and ribbing from her family had in reality only been their way of trying to figure out what was wrong? Were they just trying to *talk* to her?

How could her mom go all this time letting her believe Sue had ratted her out? Was it possible she didn't even know that Clare blamed Sue?

Clare shook her head, still having trouble grasping this. How could she have been so wrong about her family? She could only imagine all the things that she had missed out on over the years. How much fuller and richer her life would be.

She felt sick inside. She'd lost out on so much, just because she had been afraid to speak her mind.

"I thought everyone abandoned me," she told Jen. "That no one cared."

"Oh, honey." Jen rose from the chair, wrapped her arms around Clare and hugged her hard, and Clare hugged her back just as firmly. "Everyone cared. We always have. You know what this is?"

Clare sniffled and shook her head.

"This is one big cluster eff," she said, patting Clare's back. She was such a *mom*.

Clare smiled in spite of herself. "Cluster eff?"

Jen held her at arm's length and said, "I'm the mother of four boys. I have to set a good example."

"I miss the boys," Clare said. "I've missed out on so much…"

"So things will be different now."

"It might take some time to forgive Mom and Dad for lying to me." It had begun a chain reaction that left

Clare feeling isolated and alone. Like an outcast. How did you forgive someone for that?

"For what it's worth, I truly believe that they thought they were doing the right thing. They didn't want to hurt anyone. They just didn't think about the consequences of their actions."

"That doesn't make it okay."

"No, but you should talk to them about it and tell them how you feel. They won't be around forever."

Jen was right of course. Clare did need to talk to them. And her siblings needed to know what really happened. She didn't even know why she wanted to tell them. She just felt as if she needed to get it off her chest. Or maybe, after all this time, she just needed their acceptance.

"I want to tell you what happened," Clare said.

"Are you sure?"

"Very sure."

"I swear I won't tell a soul."

"No, this time I actually want you to."

Parker stood at the nurses station pretending to work on a chart, keeping his eye on the door of the break room. Clare and her sister had been in there for a while now and he was beginning to worry. Clare hadn't looked happy to see her. Things had been going so well, he hated to see something like this set them back.

"I'm sure she's fine," Rebecca said from behind the desk.

Parker turned to her. "Who?"

"Clare. You've been on edge since she went in there."

He didn't realize that he was being that obvious, or that careless. "It's complicated."

"You seem to be spending a lot more time together lately."

That was none of her business and he didn't justify it with a response.

"I'm sorry I got snippy with you," she said. "I was jealous, I guess. It's been pretty obvious that you have a thing for Clare."

"Since when?"

"Pretty much since you started at the hospital."

Had it really been that noticeable?

"I knew you and I didn't have a chance. And the truth is, you're a little old for me."

"And feeling older every day," he said, but that was okay. He felt more settled, and more content than he ever had in his life. There was no way that was a bad thing.

Convincing Clare would be another matter altogether. She was so terrified to trust this. To trust *herself*. Who knew how long it would be before she felt okay with taking their relationship to the next level. Maybe never. She was so worried about what other people would think, how they would judge her. When would she learn that it didn't matter what anyone else thought? He was in love with her. There was no other explanation for this inexorable need to protect her. He wanted to spend the rest of his life with her. He knew somewhere deep down in his soul she was the one for him. His perfect match. And he couldn't even tell her. He was paying the price for all the other people who had hurt and betrayed her.

It was frustrating as hell. And it wasn't fair. Not to her and not to him.

When Clare introduced him to her sister, his first

reaction had been to go on the defensive, and he was afraid he'd been a little rude. He was hoping to apologize to the both of them.

The break room door finally opened and Clare and her sister walked out. He could tell from where he stood that they had both been crying. But he couldn't tell if that was a good or bad thing.

Clare and her sister embraced, holding each other tight. After a moment they parted and started to walk toward him and he met them halfway. He must have looked confused, or concerned, because Clare told him immediately, "Everything is okay."

"So you'll definitely be there for dinner?" Jen asked her.

Clare smiled and nodded. "I promise."

"And you'll bring this guy along?" she asked, gesturing to Parker.

"It's a distinct possibility. If he wants to go."

"Of course he wants to go," Jen said, giving his arm a playful nudge with her elbow. "Don't you."

"Go where?" he asked.

"To meet Clare's family. There are so many of us, it can be a bit intimidating."

She wanted him to meet her family? Since when? Was it something she'd said just to placate her sister? Knowing the way they treated Clare, he wasn't sure if he wanted to meet them. It would be difficult to keep his feelings hidden.

She and her sister said goodbye, then she turned to him and smiled. "You are not going to believe what just happened to me."

Fourteen

The Texas Cattleman's Club meeting wasn't due to start for another hour, but Clare was working late and Parker was bored so he showed up early. He sat at the bar at the clubhouse, sipping his usual drink, the Family Finder app open on his phone, his profile taunting him. As it had for nearly two weeks now. It would take one tap on the screen to submit his request, but he still couldn't seem to make himself do it. Which wasn't at all like him. When he wanted something, he went after it. This time something was stopping him. The question was what.

The idea of family, and possibly one of his own, weighed heavily on his mind since the impromptu family gathering he and Clare had attended at her parents' farm this past weekend. At first she'd hemmed and hawed about bringing him, which he had tried not to take personally. He'd learned that in that sort of situation it was best to step back and let her work it out alone. If she asked for input he gave it, but trying to convince her to do something usually had her digging her heels in to do the exact opposite. But her siblings, whom she'd had a very open and honest dialogue with lately, nagged and cajoled her for a week until she finally agreed to bring him.

On the morning of the party she'd called him with the idea to bring overnight bags in case they were too tired, or more likely too hammered, to drive the hour back to Royal.

His second surprise, when they'd arrived at her parents' farm, was the sheer size of her family. He'd met countless nieces and nephews, aunts and uncles, and more cousins than should be allowed in one family. He'd tried to keep up with all the new names and faces, but somewhere around his fourth beer he'd given up. From that point on he'd addressed everyone as *sir* or *ma'am*. Even the children, who'd seemed to get a big kick out of that.

The food had been incredible, and there'd been so much of it. Roasted pig and smoked ribs and of course authentic Texas chili. Clare had told him that it was customary to bring either a side dish or dessert to share, which explained the rows and rows of platters and casserole dishes on the serving tables. There was literally enough food for a small army.

Parker had eaten himself into a food coma, and drank way more than he should have. From around dusk on, his memory had been a little spotty. He remembered a huge bonfire out in the field, and Clare's brothers joking around that they were going to throw Parker into it.

He remembered live music, and square dancing badly. Really, *really* badly. But what he remembered most was the constant smile on Clare's face, and her laugh, and how happy she'd seemed. And how sexy she'd looked when she jumped him later that night in the tent she'd borrowed from her parents. And she hadn't been exaggerating when she said her family was traditional. The fact that she and Parker were sharing a tent out of wedlock had raised a few eyebrows from the older set.

Despite his vow to never ride any breed of four-legged animal again, Clare had talked him into going horseback riding the next morning and given him a proper tour of the land. They'd stayed for a lunch of leftovers, and her mom had sent bags and bags of food home with them.

Though much of the party was a blur, he distinctly recalled thinking about his biological mother. And though meeting Clare's entire gargantuan family all at once had had him feeling a little intimidated at first, it made him realize what he had missed out on all these years. Was it possible that he had siblings somewhere, too? Would they be interested in meeting him? Did they have gatherings like Clare's family?

To find out, he would have to hit Submit. Just one tap of the mouse.

Cursing under his breath, he shut the app again.

Maybe he just wasn't ready. With everything else in his life going so well, would he only be tempting fate?

It still astounded him a little that after a lifetime of having no desire to settle down, much less have a family, he could be so sure in less than a month's time that Clare was the *one*. She was smart and sexy and fun. She challenged him emotionally and intellectually. And in the bedroom, as well. She had a sharp wit and snarky sense of humor.

She was still hesitant about their relationship going public, but they had been spending almost all of their free time together, and he knew that people were beginning to notice.

Parker heard his name called and turned to see Luc gesturing him over to a table in the back of the bar. Parker had been so lost in thought he hadn't even seen him come in. He stuck his phone in his pocket and walked over. Though Parker was far from knowing all the members of the club, he recognized the men sitting at the table with Luc. Case Baxter, who was the recently elected president of the club, and beside him Nathan Battle, the sheriff of Royal.

The men shook hands and Parker sat down, asking Luc, "How was Mexico?"

He and his wife, Julie, had just returned from a long-overdue vacation. Which had Parker thinking that maybe he and Clare should take a few days away, just the two of them.

"Hot," Luc said. "But relaxing. We got back this afternoon."

"Do anything fun?"

"We slept a lot. And caught up on our reading. Our last day there we chartered a boat."

"Sounds like the perfect vacation."

"I'd go back tomorrow if I could."

"Parker," Case said, "we were discussing the Samson Oil land grab. We still have no idea why any oil company would buy up land with no oil. Any thoughts?"

Parker shook his head. "I'm afraid I don't know

enough about the town to be much help. But I agree that it's suspicious."

"Listen and learn," Nathan said, spreading a map out across the table that marked the property the company had purchased so far, and all the land it was still trying to obtain. Parker tried to pay attention so he would appear at least slightly informed during the meeting, but his mind kept wandering.

When Case and Nathan left the bar to get ready for the meeting, Luc asked him, "Everything okay? You seem awfully distracted tonight."

"I have a lot on my mind," he said, and told Luc about his desire to meet his biological mother.

"Why now?" Luc asked.

"Let's just say that lately I've been reevaluating my priorities."

"This wouldn't have anything to do with Clare, would it?"

There was really no point in denying it. "Almost exclusively. Who told you?"

"I can tell you who didn't tell me. It's a much shorter list. If you haven't noticed by now, secrets are tough to keep in a town this small and tight-knit."

"I know." And he was okay with that. The question was how Clare would feel about it.

"I had a feeling, when you mentioned the new woman you were seeing, that it was probably Clare," Luc said. "Once you set your mind to something you don't just give up."

"I'm in love with her."

"Wow. That's the first time I've ever heard you say that."

"That's because I've never said it before. Until I met

Clare I didn't think I would ever settle down. Now I want it all. A wife and a child, or even two. I want to be everything to my kids that my father never was for me."

"Have you told her how you feel?"

"Not yet."

"What are you waiting for?"

"The right time. I'll know it when I see it."

"On the subject of marriage and family, Julie and I have a little news of our own to share. We've been throwing around the idea of starting a family for a while now, so she quit taking her birth control. We were assuming it would take at least a couple of months for her system to regulate."

"How long did it actually take?"

He grinned. "Closer to two weeks. We found out just before we left for Mexico."

Parker laughed. "Congratulations. That's great news."

He was happy for Luc, and at the same time he was a little jealous. Maybe it was time he stopped tiptoeing around the issue and told Clare how he felt. It had taken him a long time to get to this place, and he didn't want to waste a minute of it.

When Clare made it to Parker's house after work he wasn't home yet. She parked her new car in the driveway and, using the key he'd given her last week, let herself into his condo. It still felt a little strange being there alone, but he would hopefully be home soon. It had been a hellish day at work. The kind that had her questioning humanity. An unresponsive eight-month-old infant with severe brain swelling had been brought in to emergency. Though they'd done everything they could, the child had died shortly after. The worst part was that it was a textbook case of shaken-baby syndrome. The parents had been arrested, and their two other children taken by protective services. Clare had called Grace only to learn that both kids, ages two and four, had signs of abuse, as well. It was so heartbreaking that she gave herself permission to sit in the stairwell and sob, but even that didn't help much.

Clare shed her coat and dropped her purse on the cluttered coffee table, feeling depressed, her heart breaking for that poor little baby. At least she was at peace. Even if she'd survived she would have been severely mentally disabled. She probably would have spent her life in a group home, since her own parents clearly had no business raising children.

At least little Maddie's story had a happy ending. She was getting stronger every day, and would hopefully get to join her twin sister at home.

What Clare really needed was one of Parker's hugs. Feeling his arms around her somehow always managed to make the bad stuff go away for a while. Besides, she had an awful lot to be happy about these days.

She grabbed herself a beer from the fridge and flopped down on the sofa to wait for Parker.

Her relationship with her family was the best it had ever been, though things with her parents were still a little strained. It would just take her time to forgive them for lying to her. She believed that they had been truly afraid for her, and had had her best interests in mind, even though their actions had seemed to say the opposite. They had hurt her deeply, even if they hadn't meant to, and it would take a while to sort those feelings out. On the bright side, Parker had been extremely well received by her entire family, and though she'd been a bit hesitant to bring him at first, she was glad she had. For all her fears about "rich doctor" cracks, no one had said a disparaging word. And though Parker had looked thoroughly overwhelmed by the number of relatives there when they first arrived, he'd fit right in.

Only after seeing everyone all together like that had she realized how much she missed being part of a family. Before they'd left the next day her siblings had made her promise to regularly attend the monthly family dinners. She'd promised, and this time she meant it. So much had changed.

She had changed.

She'd been insistent that she and Parker continue to keep their relationship a secret, but people were beginning to put two and two together. Though no one had the guts to come right out and ask her about it, it was only a matter of time. Besides, all of her reasons for keeping it quiet seemed a little silly now. She had tried to convince herself that it would put her job in jeopardy, sleeping with the boss. But that was just a lame excuse to not let him close.

She tried putting herself in Parker's place, tried to imagine how she would feel if the tables were turned, if he wanted to keep it a secret. The truth was, it kinda sucked.

Maybe deep down she felt as if she didn't deserve someone like him, that people would see them as mismatched, and her as pathetic. She realized today, with complete certainty, that she didn't give a damn what anyone thought. She was so happy these past few weeks that sometimes she wanted to shout it from the rooftops. So tonight she planned to tell him that she wanted to take things public. She was tired of hiding, tired of watching what she said, and whom she said it in front of.

There was something else she wanted to say to him, something that she had never said to anyone but her family. The *L* word. Up to now, in her mind, love had always meant obligation, and sacrifice, and often heartbreak. It meant giving without getting anything in return.

With Parker it was different. He gave as much as he took. More even. And he must have been a saint to put up with all of her weird hang-ups and personality quirks. But without fail he accepted her for exactly who she was, no question.

Until now the only place she'd ever felt truly in her element was at work. For the first time in forever, with her family and with Parker, she felt as if she truly belonged. As if she fit in.

She heard the garage door open and her heart leaped up into her throat. Despite being with one another nearly every day, the excitement of seeing him walk through the door was a thrill that never went away. She met him at the door, greeting him with a kiss, and as his arms went around her she felt the stress of the day slipping away. She held him as tight as she could.

"If you let go for a second and let me take my coat off I could hug you properly," he teased, and she held him even tighter. "Hey, is everything okay?"

She looked up at him, into his beautiful eyes, and though she meant to tell him about her crummy day, and say how happy she was that he was home, something altogether different came out.

"I love you, Parker."

He blinked. Then blinked again. Then he grinned and said, "I love you, too, Clare."

That wasn't all that hard. And she liked that he didn't make a big deal out of it.

"How was your meeting?" she asked, loosening his tie.

"Good. Luc and Julie are expecting."

"No kidding."

"Yeah, he seems pretty excited. They want me to be the baby's doctor."

"Of course they do. You're the best."

He grinned and kissed her. "Thanks. You're not so bad yourself. How was work?"

"Not so good."

"Let me grab a beer and you can tell me about it."

They snuggled on the sofa, her head resting on his shoulder as she told him about her rotten afternoon. "It was a very stressful day."

"Do I need to pull out the coloring books?" he teased. She did in fact have a few there, as well as a set of colored pencils. But right now she just wanted to be with him.

"Are you staying over tonight?" he asked.

She should probably head home, but she didn't feel like going back out into the cold. "If you don't mind."

He gave her a *yeah right* look. "Do I ever mind when you spend the night?"

"I'm warning you, I'm too tired to do anything but sleep."

He laughed. "Okay."

"I'm serious. I'm exhausted."

"Yet somehow you always manage to find the energy."

After they finished their beers they went up to his bedroom and he switched on the news while they undressed. Then she remembered her purse was still downstairs with her phone in it.

"I left my phone downstairs," she told him. "I'm going to grab it."

He patted the pockets of his pants. "I think I left mine in the kitchen. I'm pretty sure I set it down when I was taking my coat off."

"I'll get yours, too." Her feet ached as she trudged down the stairs. She hooked her purse over her shoulder, then grabbed his phone, which was sitting on the kitchen counter. She was almost to the stairs when his phone buzzed. She glanced at the screen and saw that it was an incoming text message from Luc Wakefield.

The two-word preview on his locked screen said, About Clare...

She stopped at the bottom of the stairs. *About Clare* what? Had Parker told Luc about his relationship with Clare? Even though he *swore* he wouldn't? Or had Luc just heard about them through the hospital grapevine.

She itched to read the rest of the text, then thought about their conversation regarding his phone, and the dangers of snooping. But it probably wasn't a big deal. He wouldn't have given her his code if he had something to hide.

She tapped in the code and the text flashed on the screen.

She read it once, then read it again, then read it a third time.

Well, he'd been right about one thing. She definitely wished she'd never seen it.

Fifteen

Parker was sitting on the edge of the mattress watching CNN when something hit him hard in the back. "Ow! What the…"

He turned to see his phone lying on the blanket behind him, then he looked up to see Clare standing in the bedroom doorway. That had really hurt, not to mention that if she'd missed she might have broken his phone. "Thanks, I think."

At first he thought she was teasing him, and had just underestimated her own strength. Then he saw her face. She was wearing a look like he'd never seen before. As if someone had died. Or worse.

His heart skipped a beat. "What's wrong?"

"You got a text from Dr. Wakefield."

Uh-oh. What the hell had Luc said?

She didn't move from the doorway. "Aren't you going to read it?"

"Um, sure." He punched in his code and the text flashed on the screen.

About Clare… I know we ended the bet, but since you slept with her before that, you technically win. I'll stop by the bank on my way to work. You want that in small bills?

He cursed under his breath. Then cursed again.

"It was a bet?" she asked, her voice trembling. "You bet Luc that you would sleep with me?"

He wanted to deny it, but he couldn't.

The outrage and devastation were written all over her face, making him feel like the giant ass that he was. He tried to think of something to say, anything to make her stop looking at him like that.

"I know it sounds awful," he said. "But if you let me explain—"

"Did you or did you not bet Luc that you would sleep with me?"

Shit.

"I did. But it's not… It isn't…" He didn't even know what to say. He had no excuse, no logical explanation. He wanted to kill Luc, but this was his own fault. He'd done a bad, stupid thing and now he had to own up to it and take his lumps.

"I was going to tell you, it just never seemed like the right time."

"No, you're just a coward."

"Clare, I'm sorry."

"So am I, Parker." She turned around and he jumped up to follow her.

"Clare, wait!"

He caught up with her at the bottom of the stairs. He grabbed her arm and she violently jerked it away. "*Do not* touch me. You don't get to touch me *ever again*."

She was so furious, her face was bright red and her hands were trembling as she shoved her arms into her coat sleeves. "I am so stupid. I can't believe I let myself trust you."

"No, I'm the stupid one, Clare. And I cannot begin to tell you how sorry I am. I wasn't thinking. I didn't know—"

She raised a hand to stop him midsentence. "Save your breath, I'm not buying it. Not anymore."

She walked out the door and he let her go. She was too angry to listen to reason, even if he did have some sort of reasonable excuse. Which he didn't. He'd worked so hard to earn her trust, and in a matter of seconds he'd lost it.

Maybe she just needed time to think it through. Maybe after a day or two she would give him a chance to explain. Maybe, if he was totally honest from now on, she could learn to trust him again.

Or maybe it was just over.

Yeah, it was over.

In this day and age, with all the communications technology available, it was still possible to go radio silent and drop completely off the map. He knew because that's what Clare had done. She'd taken a week's vacation then disappeared.

Every time he let himself remember the way her face had looked when she'd walked out the door—the bitterness and hurt—his gut tied itself into knots. Which was probably why he hadn't been able to eat in two days. Nothing would go down.

Having never had a broken heart, he'd had no idea just how dreadful it could feel. He wished he could go back and apologize profusely to all of the women he'd seduced then discarded over the years. If any of them felt even a fraction of what he was feeling now…

In a word, it *sucked*.

His days of using and manipulating women to get what he wanted were officially over.

He'd left a few things at Clare's house, things he would really like to have back, like his tennis shoes, but knowing Kay had guns, he wouldn't dare. He knew how it worked in that family. He hurt Clare, so Kay would hurt him. She had brothers, too. Big ones, who could snap him like a twig, or throw him off a cliff. With all that land they had, no one would ever find the body…

But killing him would mean putting him out of his misery, and he deserved every bit of misery he was feeling. And he was sure they knew that.

He took Wednesday off and lay around the house in his pajamas flipping through the TV channels. He didn't even have anyone to talk to. Luc was the one he called with a problem. But if Parker told him it was his text that had blown everything wide-open, Luc would never forgive himself.

There was nothing on TV so he grabbed his laptop. Out of habit he clicked on the Family Finder link in his browser and the page popped up. It was times like this when having a family would come in handy.

He read through the letter section of his profile. He'd written a few short passages about himself, describing his career and his various degrees. It sounded…wrong.

Awkward or forced or something. He highlighted all the text and hit Delete. He sat for a second, looking at the blank page, wondering what it was he really wanted to impart to the woman who'd abandoned him.

He typed five words, but they pretty much said it all.

I want to meet you.

And before he could change his mind he hit Submit.

It was finally done. He'd sent it. Now all he could do was sit back and wait. He wasn't sure if he felt excited or nervous.

He wondered how long it would take—

The computer beeped as a message window popped up on his screen. I want to meet you, too.

Apparently not that long.

After exchanging phone numbers and one very short and awkward conversation, Rachel Simpson, his biological mother, had immediately purchased a plane ticket for her trip to Texas from her home in Nebraska.

Heavy traffic made him a little late picking her up, and when he walked into the baggage-claim area where they planned to meet, she was already there. Though he had never even seen a picture of her, he knew her the moment he saw her. They looked alike. And the second her eyes landed on him, it was obvious that she could see it, too.

She looked younger than he expected. But she had been only eighteen when he was born, putting her at fifty-six now.

She was very attractive—tall and slender, with long dark hair streaked with gray.

Suddenly his feet felt glued to the floor, but she came to him. And for some strange reason her uncertainty was a comfort. At least he wasn't the only one flying blind.

Then she was standing in front of him, saying, "Parker."

She held a hand out and he automatically took it, but instead of shaking it, she held it tight. "I've been looking forward to this for a very long time," she said. "It's so good to see you."

He wished he could say the same, but right now he wasn't sure how he felt. He was feeling so many things he couldn't sort them all out. All he could manage was, "How was your flight?"

"It was good. My return flight leaves in three hours. I'd have stayed longer but I couldn't get the time off work. Is there somewhere that we can go and talk?"

They chose a coffee shop close to the airport, and she asked him question after question about himself. He waited to feel some sort of connection, or affection.

"You must have questions about me," she said finally.

He did, but all he could think to say was, "You answered my request so fast."

"I've been registered on the site since it was created. I figured that if you wanted to see me, this would be one of the first places you looked."

"You could have just contacted me."

"I didn't think it would be fair to disrupt your life. I knew that you had the resources to find me if you wanted to."

"Why didn't you want me?"

His blunt question seemed to surprise her, and he surprised himself. But he had never been one to dance around an issue. He'd met with her to get answers, and he was going to get them.

"I did want you, I swear, but I was only eighteen when you were born and I had signed a contract. He told you that I was a surrogate?"

Parker nodded.

"I only agreed to do it to make money for college, but your father was so charming and sweet to me. I was very young and naive, and it was the late seventies so that sort of thing wasn't common, and not looked upon too favorably. My family would have been horrified to learn what I did. Your grandparents were very old-fashioned."

His grandparents? The ones that he hadn't even known existed? "Were?"

"They were over forty when they had my brother and me. They passed years ago."

He hoped she wasn't expecting any sympathy from him.

"So you just disappeared for nine months? Didn't your parents wonder where you were?"

"I told them that I got a job as a nanny to save money for school."

He picked up his coffee cup to take a sip, but put it back down untouched. The truth was, he felt a little sick to his stomach. "Did you love him?"

"I thought I did. I wanted to, and not just because he was rich. Though that was what everyone believed. It was wonderful at first. You know how charming he could be. He could also be cold and cruel. But by that time I wanted you so much, I was willing to stay with him."

"Yet you left."

"Parker, he didn't give me a choice. He *made* me leave."

"Was it true what he told me about the limo driver?"

"Darren was the only friend I had."

"I heard it was more than that. He said you ran off with him."

"Your father and I had a terrible fight. He was never around, and when he was, though he claimed to love me, he treated me like a subordinate."

Parker could certainly relate to that.

"Darren was just consoling me, but your father got the wrong idea. He accused me of cheating on him. He kicked me out, said I broke the terms of our agreement, and sent me away without a penny to my name. I hadn't earned the money. You were only two weeks old. I was devastated."

"What did you do?"

"The only thing I could do. I went home to Nebraska and tried to convince everyone that my heart wasn't breaking. I tried to forget."

"It would seem you did a pretty good job."

There was regret and pain in her voice when she said, "No, Parker, I haven't. In thirty-eight years a day hasn't passed that I didn't think of you, and wonder what you were doing."

"But you didn't try to see me."

"I signed a contract saying I wouldn't. And at the time I thought I was doing the right thing. I thought that he could give you a better life than I ever could. But once I got to know him, when I realized how wrong I was about him, it was too late."

"I'm no attorney, but I'm fairly certain that any contract would become null and void the day I turned eighteen. Yet here we are *twenty* years later."

She winced, as if his words actually stung, and he felt a stab of guilt. "As I said, I didn't want to disrupt your life. I felt as if I had no right."

"Because thinking that you abandoned me for the limo driver was so much better."

"You have every reason to be angry. And I will never forgive myself for robbing you of the opportunity to be a part of our family."

"Family?"

"You have two brother and two sisters. You also have seven nieces and nephews. Your brother David is thirty-five. He's a country vet. He has three boys. Jeanie is thirty-two. She's a schoolteacher, and she has four children. Two of each. Now, the twins, Aaron and Ashley, came along later. They graduate high school next year."

It was hard to imagine that he could have a brother and sister still in high school. The whole situation was making him feel weirdly left out. And resentful. "Do they know about me?"

"They do. And they would have all flown here with me if I let them. They can't wait to meet you. If that's something you want."

He didn't know what he wanted. He just felt angry and annoyed. "Did your husband know about me?"

She nodded. "It took me years to work up the courage to tell him. But he was one hundred percent supportive. He was a good man, Parker. A good father. I wish you could have known him."

"He's not…?"

"He passed away last year. Lung cancer."

It was so much to take in all at once. There were years' and years' worth of things he'd missed.

"There's something else that you need to know," she said, her tone ominous. "Something you probably don't know about your father. He was sterile. He couldn't have children of his own."

"So how am I here?"

"I was already pregnant when I met him."

Sixteen

The coffee shop spun around him. Of all scenarios he had imagined over the years regarding his mother, this had never even crossed his mind. But it sure did explain a lot. Why he and the man he thought was his father were so completely different. Somewhere deep down Parker had always felt an odd detachment from his father. Now he knew why.

"So who is my real father?"

She wrapped her hands around her coffee cup looking so sad. "I didn't know him very well. I had just graduated high school and we were on vacation. Every summer my parents would rent a cabin at the lake and we would spend a month there. Your father's name was Michael Johnson. He was eighteen, and on vacation with his grandparents. He had joined the army and was leaving for boot camp as soon as their vacation was over. It was love at first sight for both of us. We were inseparable for two weeks. We spent every second we could together. I was back in Nebraska when I discovered I was pregnant."

"Did you try to contact him?"

"He was in basic training by then. I didn't have a clue *how* to get in touch with him, and by the time I found him, it was too late. He was dead."

So his biological father was dead.

He wanted to feel remorse, or regret, or pride, but he just felt numb. "How did he die?"

"I don't know much, only that he was on a rescue mission and the helicopter he was in was shot down. Everyone on board was killed. He died a hero."

That meant more to him than she could possibly understand. Since his father—the man who raised him— had never done a decent thing in his life.

"I've used the internet to follow your career over the years," she told him. "I know this probably doesn't mean much, but I'm so proud of the man you've become."

His laugh was a bitter one. "Don't believe everything you read. The truth is, I'm a screw-up."

The sympathy in her eyes nearly did him in. She really cared. "Do you want to talk about it?"

Though he hadn't planned to bring up his relationship with Clare, or anything else about his life, he heard himself spilling his guts. And once he got started, he couldn't seem to stop. He told her the entire sordid story.

"She sounds very special," his mother said when he was all talked out. "What are you planning to do to get her back?"

"There's nothing I can do," he said. "I betrayed her trust. It's over."

"But you love her, don't you? And she loves you?"

He nodded. "Or she used to."

"Then you have to at least try." She laid a hand over his and squeezed gently, and in that instant he felt a connection. A sense of familiarity. It was…nice. So he left his hand there. "Trust me when I say people don't fall out of love overnight. She probably just needs time to sort things out."

"You have no idea how stubborn she is."

"It sounds to me as if you're a little stubborn, too. Or you're just afraid of being rejected again."

Maybe she was right. He'd never been rejected before, so he had no idea how to handle it, or what to do to get her back. He was stumbling around in the dark, and his instincts were failing him.

"Okay," he said, "tell me what I should do. How I can fix this."

"Parker, only you know the answer to that question."

But that was the problem. He didn't. "I don't even know where she is."

"Don't you?"

Of course he did. She was at her parents' ranch. But talking to her meant going there and facing her entire family.

Jesus. Clare was right. He really was a coward.

He and Rachel talked up until the minute it was time to take her back to the airport, and all the way to the terminal, where he dropped her outside the doors. They parted with a promise that they would keep in touch, and he gave her permission to give his contact information to his brothers and sisters.

He drove home, weighing his options, and he realized Rachel was right. Clare was worth fighting for.

And if he failed, he would live the rest of his life regretting it. But at least he could say that he'd tried. He would stop home and pick up a few things, then drive to her parents' farm. If she refused to talk to him, he would camp out with the horses until she changed her mind. He would even take on her brothers if he had to. He was willing to go to any lengths to get her back.

But when he pulled down his street, her car was in his driveway and he felt a rush of hope that made his scalp tingle.

He hit the brake and stopped in the road. He had planned to use the hour's drive to the farm to figure out what he was going to say to her. It looked as if he would have to wing it.

He pulled in beside her car. She wasn't in it. Then he remembered that she still had his key. He shuddered to think what she might be doing in there. Setting his house on fire maybe?

He parked in the garage, then let himself inside, nerves roiling in his belly. He hadn't been this nervous, or this determined, in his life. She may have been stubborn, but so was he, and he refused to let her leave until he'd had the chance to explain.

She was sitting on the sofa, and the deep love and respect that he felt for her propelled him forward when what he really wanted to do was turn around and run. Never in his adult life had he been intimidated by a woman, but Clare scared the hell out of him right now.

As he walked into the room she stood. She didn't say a word; she just looked at him, her expression blank. And he couldn't think of a damned thing to say. He stood there, trying to make his brain work.

She walked over, until she was standing in front of

him. She had her hair up in one of those messy buns, and he itched to pull the band out so it would tumble out over her shoulders.

For several excruciating seconds she just looked at him. Searching his face. He waited for her to punch him, or scratch his eyes out. Instead, she threw her arms around him.

He was so stunned that for a second he just stood there, speechless.

"I'm so sorry," she said, laying her cheek against his chest, holding him so tight.

Wait a minute. Had she really just apologized to *him*?

"Clare, you have nothing to be sorry for. I betrayed your trust. I'm the bad guy here."

She looked up at him. "And I betrayed yours."

He blinked. What the hell was she talking about? "I don't understand."

"I said I loved you, and at the first sign of trouble I exploded. I didn't even give you a chance to explain. I was so wrapped up in my own feelings I didn't even stop to think about yours."

"Clare, this was my fault."

"Not completely. I should have been more understanding. I was just scared, and feeling vulnerable."

"You had every right to be. I screwed up."

"And I forgive you."

He blinked. "Just like that?"

"You made a mistake."

"It was a stupid move. I don't even know what I was thinking. I guess I wasn't."

"After all the soul-searching you've done, and the changes you've made, you were bound to have a setback and do something the old Parker would have done.

But I'm not in love with that guy. I'm in love with you, right now, just the way you are."

"I never meant to hurt you. And I was a coward for not telling you about the bet. It was stupid and childish."

"And I'm sorry that I overreacted so badly. And I don't want to fight. I want to fix this. Fix me."

"There's nothing to fix," he said, pulling her close and holding her tight, hardly able to conceive that she was giving him a second chance. "You're perfect."

"Far from it." She rose up on her toes and kissed him gently. "All I know is that I love you, and the past few days I've been miserable without you. The idea that I might never kiss you again, or feel your arms around me..." Her voice wavered and tears swam in her eyes. "We can figure this out."

"Yes," he said, "I want that, too."

She cupped his face in her hands, smiled up at him. "I really love you, Parker. So much."

"I love you, too. And I have so much to tell you. I met my mother today."

Clare gasped and her eyes lit. "You did?"

"You're not the only one with a big family. Turns out I have two half brothers and two half sisters. But we can talk about that later. Right now I just want to hold you."

After another long and wonderful embrace, she looked up at him and said, "I was thinking that since you won the bet because of me, it would only be fair to give me half of the prize."

"You can have it all," he said, letting go of her so he could take out his wallet. He pulled out a ten-dollar bill and handed it to her.

She looked at the bill, then back to him. "Ten bucks?"

"Yup."

"That's it?"

"'Fraid so. They're not serious bets. We always goof around."

She laughed, and shook her head, and it was the most beautiful thing he'd ever heard. They were okay. And he was never letting her go again.

"You know, this is all Maddie's fault," he said.

Clare looked at him funny. "Why do you say that?"

"Sharing in her care brought us together in a way no other patient has before. It's because of her that we connected."

"That's true," she said. "Remind me to thank her someday."

"I know things moved pretty fast with us, and to ask you to marry me right this minute would be pushing it."

"A little," she agreed.

"I just want you to know that I have every intention of spending the rest of my life with you. Whether you like it or not."

She grinned. "I think I like it."

"I don't care if we wait ten years to get married, as long as I know I have your heart." He cradled her face in his hands, kissed her gently. "Because, cupcake, you definitely have mine."

* * * * *

Don't miss a single installment of
TEXAS CATTLEMAN'S CLUB:
LIES AND LULLABIES
Baby Secrets and a Scheming Sheikh Rock
Royal, Texas

COURTING THE COWBOY BOSS
by USA TODAY *bestselling author Janice Maynard*

LONE STAR HOLIDAY PROPOSAL
by USA TODAY *bestselling author Yvonne Lindsay*

NANNY MAKES THREE
by Cat Schield

THE DOCTOR'S BABY DARE
by USA TODAY *bestselling author Michelle Celmer*

THE SEAL'S SECRET HEIRS
by Kat Cantrell

A SURPRISE FOR THE SHEIKH
by Sarah M. Anderson

IN PURSUIT OF HIS WIFE
by Kristi Gold

A BRIDE FOR THE BOSS
by USA TODAY *bestselling author Maureen Child*

If you're on Twitter, tell us what you think of
Harlequin Desire! #harlequindesire

NEVER TOO LATE

Brenda Jackson

Chapter 1

Twelve days and counting...

Pushing a lock of twisted hair that had fallen in her face behind her ear, Sienna Bradford, soon to become Sienna Davis once again, straightened her shoulders as she walked into the cabin she'd once shared with her husband—soon-to-be ex-husband.

She glanced around. Had it been just three years ago when Dane had brought her here for the first time? Three years ago when the two of them had sat there in front of the fireplace after making love, and planned their wedding? Promising that no matter what, their marriage would last forever? She took a deep breath knowing that for them, forever would end in twelve days in Judge Ratcliff's chambers.

Just thinking about it made her heart ache, but she decided it wouldn't help matters to have a pity party.

What was done was done and things just hadn't worked out between her and Dane like they'd hoped. There was nothing to do now but move on with her life. But first, according to a letter her attorney had received from Dane's attorney a few days ago, she had ten days to clear out any and all of her belongings from the cabin, and the sooner she got the task done, the better. Dane had agreed to let her keep the condo if she returned full ownership of the cabin to him. She'd had no problem with that, since he had owned it before they married.

Sienna crossed the room, shaking off the March chill. According to forecasters, a snowstorm was headed toward the Smoky Mountains within the next seventy-two hours, which meant she had to hurry and pack up her stuff and take the two-hour drive back to Charlotte. Once she got home she intended to stay inside and curl up in bed with a good book. Sienna smiled, thinking that a "do nothing" weekend was just what she needed in her too frantic life.

Her smile faded when she considered that since starting her own interior decorating business a year and a half ago, she'd been extremely busy—and she had to admit that was when her marital problems with Dane had begun.

Sienna took a couple of steps toward the bedroom to begin packing her belongings when she heard the sound of the door opening. Turning quickly, she suddenly remembered she had forgotten to lock the door. Not smart when she was alone in a secluded cabin high up in the mountains, and a long way from civilization.

A scream quickly died in her throat when the person who walked in—standing a little over six feet with dark eyes, close-cropped black hair, chestnut coloring and a medium build—was none other than her soon-to-be ex.

From the glare on his face, she could tell he wasn't happy to see her. But so what? She wasn't happy to see him, either, and couldn't help wondering why he was there.

Before she could swallow the lump in her throat to ask, he crossed his arms over his broad chest, intensified his glare and said in that too sexy voice she knew so well, "I thought that was your car parked outside, Sienna. What are you doing here?"

Chapter 2

Dane wet his suddenly dry lips and immediately decided he needed a beer. Lucky for him there was a six-pack in the refrigerator from the last time he'd come to the cabin. But he didn't intend on moving an inch until Sienna told him what she was doing there.

She was nervous, he could tell. Well, that was too friggin bad. She was the one who'd filed for the divorce—he hadn't. But since she had made it clear that she wanted him out of her life, he had no problem giving her what she wanted, even if the pain was practically killing him. But she'd never know that.

"What do you think I'm doing here?" she asked smartly, reclaiming his absolute attention.

"If I knew, I wouldn't have asked," he said, giving her the same unblinking stare. And to think that at one time he actually thought she was his whole world. At some point during their marriage she had changed and transitioned into quite a character—someone he was certain he didn't know anymore.

She met his gaze for a long, level moment before placing her hands on her hips. Doing so drew his attention to her body; a body he'd seen naked countless times, a body he knew as well as his own; a body he used to ease into during the heat of passion to receive pleasure so keen and satisfying, just thinking about it made him hard.

"The reason I'm here, Dane Bradford, is because your attorney sent mine this nasty little letter demanding that I remove my stuff within ten days, and this weekend was better than next weekend. However, no thanks to you, I still had to close the shop early to beat traffic and the bad weather."

He actually smiled at the thought of her having to do that. "And I bet it almost killed you to close your shop early. Heaven forbid. You probably had to cancel a couple of appointments. Something I could never get you to do for me."

Sienna rolled her eyes. They'd had this same argument over and over again and it all boiled down to the same thing. He thought her job meant more to her than he did because of all the time she'd put into it. But what really irked her with that accusation was that before she'd even entertained the idea of quitting her job and embarking on her own business, they had talked about it and what it would mean. She would have to work her butt off and network to build a new clientele; and then there would be time spent working on decorating proposals, spending long hours in many beautiful homes of the rich and famous. And he had understood and had been supportive…at least in the beginning.

But then he began complaining that she was spending too much time away from home, away from him. Things only got worse from there, and now she was a woman who had gotten married at twenty-four and was getting divorced at twenty-seven.

"Look, Dane, it's too late to look back, reflect and complain. In twelve days you'll be free of me and I'll be free of you. I'm sure there's a woman out there who has the time and patience to—"

"Now, that's a word you don't know the meaning of, Sienna," Dane interrupted. "*Patience*. You were always in a rush, and your tolerance level for the least little thing was zero. Yeah, I know I probably annoyed the hell out of you at times. But then there were times you annoyed me, as well. Neither of us is perfect."

Sienna let out a deep breath. "I never said I was perfect, Dane."

"No, but you sure as hell acted like you thought you were, didn't you?"

Chapter 3

Dane's question struck a nerve. Considering her background, how could he assume Sienna thought she was perfect? She had come from a dysfunctional family if ever there was one. Her mother hadn't loved her father, her father loved all women except her mother, and neither seemed to love their only child. Sienna had always combated lack of love with doing the right thing, thinking that if she did, her parents would eventually love her. It didn't work. But still, she had gone through high school and college being the good girl, thinking being good would eventually pay off and earn her the love she'd always craved.

In her mind, it had when she'd met Dane, the man least likely to fall in love with her. He was the son of the millionaire Bradfords who'd made money in land development. She hadn't been his family's choice and they made sure she knew it every chance they got. Whenever she was around them, they made her feel inadequate, like she didn't measure up to their society friends, and since she didn't come from a family with a prestigious background, she wasn't good enough for their son.

She bet they wished they'd never hired the company she'd been working for to decorate their home. That's how she and Dane had met. She'd been going over fabric swatches with his mother and he'd walked in after playing a game of tennis. The rest was history. But the question of the hour was: Had she been so busy trying to succeed the past year and a half, trying to be the perfect business owner, that she eventually alienated the one person who'd mattered most to her?

"Can't answer that. Can you?" Dane said, breaking into her thoughts. "Maybe that will give you something to think about twelve days from now when you put your John Hancock on the divorce papers. Now if you'll excuse me, I have something to do," he said, walking around her toward the bedroom.

"Wait. You never said why *you're* here!"

He stopped. The intensity of his gaze sent shivers of heat through her entire body. And it didn't help matters that he was wearing jeans and a dark brown leather bomber jacket that made him look sexy as hell... as usual. "I was here a couple of weekends ago and left something behind. I came to get it."

"Were you alone?" The words rushed out before she could hold them back and immediately she wanted to smack herself. The last thing she wanted was for him to think she cared...even if she did.

He hooked his thumbs in his jeans and continued to hold her gaze. "Would it matter to you if I weren't?"

She couldn't look at him, certain he would see her

lie when she replied, "No, it wouldn't matter. What you do is none of my business."

"That's what I thought." And then he walked off toward the bedroom and closed the door.

Sienna frowned. That was another thing she didn't like about Dane. He never stayed around to finish one of their arguments. Thanks to her parents she was a pro at it, but Dane would always walk away after giving some smart parting remark that only made her that much more angry. He didn't know how to fight fair. He didn't know how to fight at all. He'd come from a family too dignified for such nonsense.

Moving toward the kitchen to see if there was anything of hers in there, Sienna happened to glance out the window.

"Oh, my God," she said, rushing over to the window. It was snowing already. No, it wasn't just snowing… There was a full-scale blizzard going on outside. What happened to the seventy-two-hour warning?

She heard Dane when he came out of the bedroom. He looked beyond her and out the window, uttering one hell of a curse word before quickly walking to the door, slinging it open and stepping outside.

In just that short period of time, everything was beginning to turn white. The last time they'd had a sudden snowstorm such as this had been a few years ago. It had been so bad the media had nicknamed it the "Beast from the East."

It seemed the Beast was back and it had turned downright spiteful. Not only was it acting ugly outside, it had placed Sienna in one hell of a predicament. She was stranded in a cabin in the Smoky Mountains with her soon-to-be ex. Things couldn't get any more bizarre than that.

Chapter 4

Moments later, when Dane stepped back into the cabin, slamming the door behind him, Sienna could tell he was so mad he could barely breathe.

"What's wrong, Dane? You being forced to cancel a date tonight?" she asked snidely. A part of her was still upset at the thought that he might have brought someone here a couple of weekends ago when they weren't officially divorced yet. The mere fact they had been separated for six months didn't count. She hadn't gone out with anyone. Indulging in a relationship with another man hadn't even crossed her mind.

He took a step toward her and she refused to back up. She was determined to maintain her ground and her composure, although the intense look in his eyes was causing crazy things to happen to her body, like it normally did whenever they were alone for any period of time. There may have been a number of things wrong with their marriage, but lack of sexual chemistry had never been one of them.

"Do you know what this means?" he asked, his voice shaking in anger.

She tilted her head to one side. "Other than I'm being forced to remain here with you for a couple of hours, no, I don't know what it means."

She saw his hands ball into fists at his sides and knew he was probably fighting the urge to strangle her. "We're not talking about hours, Sienna. Try days. Haven't you been listening to the weather reports?"

She glared at him. "Haven't you? I'm not here by myself."

"Yes, but I thought I could come up here and in ten minutes max get what I came for, and leave before the bad weather kicked in."

Sienna regretted that she hadn't been listening to the weather reports, at least not in detail. She'd known that a snowstorm was headed toward the mountains within seventy-two hours, which was why she'd thought, like Dane, that she had time to rush and get in and out before the nasty weather hit. Anything other than that, she was clueless. And what was he saying about them being up here for days instead of hours? "Yes, I did listen to the weather reports, but evidently I missed something."

He shook his head. "Evidently you missed a lot, if you think this storm is going to blow over in a couple of hours. According to forecasters, what you see isn't the worst of it, and because of that unusual cold front hovering about in the east, it may last for days."

She swallowed deeply. The thought of spending *days*

alone in a cabin with Dane didn't sit well with her. "How many days are we talking about?"

"Try three or four."

She didn't want to try any at all, and as she continued to gaze into his eyes she saw a look of worry replace the anger in their dark depths. Then she knew what had him upset.

"Do we have enough food and supplies up here to hold us for three or four days?" she asked, as she began to nervously gnaw on her lower lip. The magnitude of the situation they were in was slowly dawning on her, and when he didn't answer immediately she knew they were in trouble.

Chapter 5

Dane saw the panic that suddenly lined Sienna's face. He wished he could say he didn't give a damn, but there was no way that he could. This woman would always matter to him whether she was married to him or not. From the moment he had walked into his father's study that day and their gazes had connected, he had known then, as miraculous at it had seemed, and without a word spoken between them, that he was meant to love her. And for a while he had convinced her of that, but not anymore. Evidently, at some point during their marriage, she began believing otherwise.

"Dane?"

He rubbed his hand down his face, trying to get his thoughts together. Given the situation they were in, he knew honesty was foremost. But then he'd always been honest with her, however, he doubted she could say the same for herself. "To answer your question, Sienna, I'm not sure. Usually I keep the place well stocked of everything, but like I said earlier, I was here a couple of weekends ago, and I used a lot of the supplies then."

He refused to tell her that in a way it had been her fault. Receiving those divorce papers had driven him here, to wallow in self-pity, vent out his anger and drink his pain away with a bottle of Johnny Walker Red. "I guess we need to go check things out," he said, trying not to get as worried as she was beginning to look.

He followed her into the kitchen, trying not to watch the sway of her hips as she walked in front of him. The hot, familiar sight of her in a pair of jeans and pullover sweater had him cursing under his breath and summoning up a quick remedy for the situation he found himself in. The thought of being stranded for any amount of time with Sienna wasn't good.

He stopped walking when she flung open the refrigerator. His six-pack of beer was still there, but little else. But then he wasn't studying the contents of the refrigerator as much as he was studying her. She was bent over, looking inside, but all he could think of was another time he had walked into this kitchen and found her in that same position, and wearing nothing more than his T-shirt that had barely covered her bottom. It hadn't taken much for him to go into a crazed fit of lust and quickly remove his pajama bottoms and take her right then and there, against the refrigerator, giving them both the orgasm of a lifetime.

"Thank goodness there are some eggs in here," she said, intruding on his heated thoughts down memory lane. "About half a dozen. And there's a loaf of bread that looks edible. There's some kind of meat in the freezer, but I'm not sure what it is, though. Looks like chicken."

She turned around and her pouty mouth tempted him to kiss it, devour it and make her moan. He watched her sigh deeply and then she gave him a not-so-hopeful gaze and said, "Our rations don't look good, Dane. What are we going to do?"

Chapter 6

Sienna's breath caught when the corners of Dane's mouth tilted in an irresistible smile. She'd seen the look before. She knew that smile and she also recognized that bulge pressing against his zipper. She frowned. "Don't even think it, Dane."

He leaned back against the kitchen counter. Hell, he wanted to do more than think it, he wanted to do it. But, of course, he would pretend he hadn't a clue as to what she was talking about. "What?"

Her frown deepened. "And don't act all innocent with me. I know what you were thinking."

A smile tugged deeper at Dane's lips knowing she probably did. There were some things a man couldn't hide and a rock-solid hard-on was one of them. He decided not to waste his time and hers pretending the chemistry between them was dead when they both knew it was still very much alive. "Don't ask me to apologize. It's not my fault you have so much sex appeal and my desire for you is automatic, even when we're headed for divorce court."

Dane saying the word "*divorce*" was a stark reminder that their life together, as they once knew it, would be over in twelve days. "Let's get back to important matters, Dane, like our survival. On a positive note, we might be able to make due if we cut back on meals, which may be hard for you with your ferocious appetite."

A wicked sounding chuckle poured from his throat. "Which one?"

Sienna swallowed as her pulse pounded in response to Dane's question. She was quickly reminded, although she wished there was some way she could forget, that her husband...or soon-to-be ex...did have two appetites. One was of a gastric nature and the other purely sexual. Thoughts of the purely sexual one had intense heat radiating all through her. Dane had devoured every inch of her body in ways she didn't even want to think about. Especially now.

She placed her hands on her hips knowing he was baiting her; really doing a hell of a lot more than that. He was stirring up feelings inside her that were making it hard for her to think straight. "Get serious, Dane."

"I am." He then came to stand in front of her. "Did you bring anything with you?"

She lifted a brow. "Anything like what?"

"Stuff to snack on. You're good for that. How you do it without gaining a pound is beyond me."

She shrugged, refusing to tell him that she used to work it off with all those in-bed, out-of-bed exercises they used to do. If he hadn't noticed then she wouldn't tell him that in six months without him in her bed, she had gained five pounds. "I might have a candy bar or two in the car."

He smiled. "That's all?"

She rolled her eyes upward. "Okay, okay, I might have a couple of bags of chips, too." She decided not to mention the three boxes of Girl Scout cookies that had been purchased that morning from a little girl standing in front of a grocery store.

"I hadn't planned to spend the night here, Dane. I had merely thought I could quickly pack things and leave."

He nodded. "Okay, I'll get the snacks from your car while I'm outside checking on some wood we'll need for the fire. The power is still on, but I can't see that lasting too much longer. I wished I would have gotten that generator fixed."

Her eyes widened in alarm. "You didn't?"

"No. So you might want to go around and gather up all the candles you can. And there should be a box of matches in one of these drawers."

"Okay."

Dane turned to leave. He then turned back around. She was nibbling on her bottom lip as he assumed she would be. "And stop worrying. We're going to make it."

When he walked out the room, Sienna leaned back against the closed refrigerator, thinking those were the exact words he'd said to her three years ago when he had asked her to marry him. Now she *was* worried because they didn't have a proved track record.

Chapter 7

After putting on the snow boots he kept at the cabin, Dane made his way out the doors, grateful for the time he wouldn't be in Sienna's presence. Being around her and still loving her like he did was hard. Even now he didn't know the reason for the divorce, other than what was noted in the papers he'd been served that day a few weeks ago. Irreconcilable differences...whatever the hell that was supposed to mean.

Sienna hadn't come to him so they could talk about any problems they were having. He had come home one day and she had moved out. He still was at a loss as to what could have been so wrong with their marriage that she could no longer see a future for them.

He would always recall that time as being the lowest point in his life. For days it was as if a part of him was missing. It had taken a while to finally pull himself together and realize she wasn't coming back no matter how many times he'd asked her to. And all it took was the receipt of that divorce petition to make him realize that Sienna wanted him out of her life, and actually believed that whatever issues kept them apart couldn't be resolved.

A little while later Dane had gathered more wood to put with the huge stack already on the back porch, glad that at least, if nothing else, they wouldn't freeze to death. The cabin was equipped with enough toiletries to hold them for at least a week, which was a good thing. And he hadn't wanted to break the news to Sienna that the meat in the freezer wasn't chicken, but deer meat that one of his clients had given him a couple of weeks ago after a hunting trip. It was good to eat, but he knew Sienna well enough to know she would have to be starving before she would consume any of it.

After rubbing his icy hands on his jeans, he stuck them into his pockets to keep them from freezing. Walking around the house, he strolled over to her car, opened the door and found the candy bars, chips and… Girl Scout cookies, he noted, lifting a brow. She hadn't mentioned them, and he saw they were her favorite kind, as well as his. He quickly recalled the first year they were married and how they shared the cookies as a midnight snack after making love. He couldn't help but smile as he remembered that night and others where they had spent time together, not just in bed but cooking in the kitchen, going to movies, concerts, parties, having picnics and just plain sitting around and talking for hours.

He suddenly realized that one of the things that had been missing from their marriage for a while was communication. When had they stopped talking? The first thought that grudgingly came to mind was when she'd begun bringing work home, letting it intrude on what had always been their time together. That's when they had begun living in separate worlds.

Dane breathed in deeply. He wanted to get back into Sienna's world and he definitely wanted her back in his. He didn't want a divorce. He wanted to keep his wife but he refused to resort to any type of manipulating, dominating or controlling tactics to do it. What he and Sienna needed was to use this weekend to keep it honest and talk openly about what had gone wrong with their marriage. They would go further by finding ways to resolve things. He still loved her and wanted to believe that deep down she still loved him.

There was only one way to find out.

Chapter 8

Sienna glanced around the room seeing all the lit candles and thinking just how romantic they made the cabin look. Taking a deep breath, she frowned in irritation, thinking that romance should be the last thing on her mind. Dane was her soon-to-be ex-husband. Whatever they once shared was over, done with, had come to a screeching end.

If only the memories weren't so strong...

She glanced out the window and saw him piling wood on the back porch. Never in her wildest dreams would she have thought her day would end up this way, with her and Dane being stranded together at the cabin—a place they always considered as their favorite getaway spot. During the first two years of their marriage, they would come here every chance they got, but in the past year she could recall them coming only

once. Somewhere along the way she had stopped allow-
ing them time even for this.

She sighed deeply, recalling how important it had
been to her at the beginning of their marriage for them
to make time to talk about matters of interest, whether
trivial or important. They had always been attuned to
each other, and Dane had always been a good listener,
which to her conveyed a sign of caring and respect. But
the last couple of times they had tried to talk ended up
with them snapping at each other, which only built bitterness and resentment.

The lights blinked and she knew they were about
to go out. She was glad that she had taken the initia-
tive to go into the kitchen and scramble up some eggs
earlier. And she was inwardly grateful that if she had
to get stranded in the cabin during a snowstorm that
Dane was here with her. Heaven knows she would have
been a basket case had she found herself up here alone.

The lights blinked again before finally going out,
but the candles provided the cabin with plenty of light.
Not sure if the temperatures outside would cause the
pipes to freeze, she had run plenty of water in the bathtub and kitchen sink, and filled every empty jug with
water for them to drink. She'd also found batteries to
put in the radio so they could keep up with any reports
on the weather.

"I saw the lights go out. Are you okay?"

Sienna turned around. Dane was leaning in the doorway with his hands stuck in the pockets of his jeans.
The pose made him look incredibly sexy. "Yes, I'm
okay. I was able to get the candles all lit and there are
plenty more."

"That's good."

"Just in case the pipes freeze and we can't use the shower, I filled the bathtub up with water so we can take a bath that way." At his raised brow she quickly added, "Separately, of course. And I made sure I filled plenty of bottles of drinking water, too."

He nodded. "Sounds like you've been busy."

"So have you. I saw through the window when you put all that wood on the porch. It will probably come in handy."

He moved away from the door. "Yes, and with the electricity out I need to go ahead and get the fire started."

Sienna swallowed as she watched him walk toward her on his way to the fireplace, and not for the first time she thought about how remarkably handsome he was. He had that certain charisma that made women get hot all over just looking at him.

It suddenly occurred to her that he'd already got a fire started, and the way it was spreading through her was about to make her burst into flames.

Chapter 9

"You okay?" Dane asked Sienna as he walked toward her with a smile.

She nodded and cleared her throat. "Yes, why do you ask?"

"Because you're looking at me funny."

"Oh." She was vaguely aware of him walking past her to kneel in front of the fireplace. She turned and watched him, saw him move the wood around before taking a match and lighting it to start a fire. He was so good at kindling things, whether wood or the human body.

"If you like, I can make something for dinner," she decided to say, otherwise she would continue to stand there and say nothing while staring at him. It was hard trying to be normal in a rather awkward situation.

"What are our options?" he asked without looking around.

She chuckled. "An egg sandwich and tea. I made both earlier before the power went off."

He turned at that and his gaze caught hers. A smile crinkled his eyes. "Do I have a choice?"

"Not if you want to eat."

"What about those Girl Scout cookies I found in your car?"

Her eyes narrowed. "They're off-limits. You can have one of the candy bars, but the cookies are mine."

His mouth broke into a wide grin. "You have enough cookies to share, so stop being selfish."

He turned back around and she made a face at him behind his back. He was back to stoking the fire and her gaze went to his hands. Those hands used to be the givers of so much pleasure and almost ran neck and neck with his mouth…but not quite. His mouth was in a class by itself. But still, she could recall those same hands, gentle, provoking, moving all over her body; touching her everywhere and doing things to her that mere hands weren't suppose to do. However, she never had any complaints.

"Did you have any plans for tonight, Sienna?"

His words intruded into her heated thoughts. "No, why?"

"Just wondering. You thought I had a date tonight. What about you?"

She shrugged. "No. As far as I'm concerned, until we sign those final papers, I'm still legally married and wouldn't feel right going out with someone."

He turned around and locked his eyes with hers. "I know what you mean," he said. "I wouldn't feel right going out with someone else."

Heat seeped through her every pore with his words. "So you haven't been dating, either?"

"No."

There were a number of questions she wanted to ask him—how he spent his days, his nights, what his family thought of their pending divorce, what he thought of it, was he ready for it to be over for them to go their separate ways—but there was no way she could ask him any of those things. "I guess I'll go put dinner on the table."

He chuckled. "An egg sandwich and tea?"

"Yes." She turned to leave.

"Sienna?"

She turned back around. "Yes?"

"I don't like being stranded, but since I am, I'm glad it's with you."

For a moment she couldn't say anything, then she cleared her throat while backing up a couple of steps. "Ah, yeah right, same here." She backed up some more then said, "I'll go set out the food now." And then she turned and quickly left the room.

Chapter 10

Sienna glanced up when she heard Dane walk into the kitchen and smiled. "Your feast awaits you."

"Whoopee."

She laughed. "Hey, I know the feeling. I'm glad I had a nice lunch today in celebration. I took on a new client."

Dane came and joined her at the table. "Congratulations."

"Thank you."

She took a bite of her scrambled egg sandwich and a sip of her tea and then said, "It's been a long time since you seemed genuinely pleased with my accomplishments."

He glanced up after taking a sip of his own tea and stared at her for a moment. "I know and I'm sorry about that. It was hard being replaced by your work, Sienna."

She lifted her head and stared at him, met his gaze.

She saw the tightness of his jaw and the firm set of his mouth. He actually believed that something could replace him with her and knowing that hit a raw and sensitive nerve. "My work never replaced you, Dane. Why did you begin feeling that way?"

Dane leaned back in his chair, tilted his head slightly. He was more than mildly surprised with her question. It was then he realized that she really didn't know. Hadn't a clue. This was the opportunity that he wanted; what he was hoping they would have. Now was the time to put aside anger, bitterness, foolish pride and whatever else was working at destroying their marriage. Now was the time for complete honesty. "You started missing dinner. Not once but twice, sometimes three times a week. Eventually, you stopped making excuses and didn't show up."

What he'd said was the truth. "But I was working and taking on new clients," she defended. "You said you would understand."

"And I did for a while and up to a point. But there is such a thing as common courtesy and mutual respect, Sienna. In the end I felt like I'd been thrown by the wayside, that you didn't care anymore about us, our love or our marriage."

She narrowed her eyes. "And why didn't you say something?"

"When? I was usually asleep when you got home and when I got up in the morning you were too sleepy to discuss anything. I invited you to lunch several times, but you couldn't fit me into your schedule."

"I had appointments."

"Yes, and I always felt because of it that your clients were more important."

"Still, I wished you would have let me know how you felt," she said, after taking another sip of tea.

"I did, several times. But you weren't listening."

She sighed deeply. "We used to know how to communicate."

"Yes, at one time we did, didn't we?" Dane said quietly. "But I'm also to blame for the failure of our marriage, our lack of communication. And then there were the problems you were having with my parents. When it came to you, I never hesitated letting my parents know when they were out of line and that I wouldn't put up with their treatment of you. But then I felt that at some point you needed to start believing that what they thought didn't matter and stand up to them.

"I honestly thought I was doing the right thing when I decided to just stay out of it and give you the chance to deal with them, to finally put them in their place. Instead, you let them erode away at your security and confidence to the point where you felt you had to prove you were worthy of them…and of me. That's what drove you to be so successful, wasn't it, Sienna? Feeling the need to prove something is what working all those long hours was all about, wasn't it?"

Chapter 11

Sienna quickly got up from the table and walked to the window. It was turning dark but she could clearly see that things hadn't let up. It was still snowing outside, worse than an hour before. She tried to concentrate on what was beyond that window and not on the question Dane had asked her.

"Sienna?"

Moments later she turned back around to face Dane, knowing he was waiting on her response. "What do you want me to say, Dane? Trust me, you don't want to get me started since you've always known how your family felt about me."

His brow furrowed sharply as he moved from the table to join her at the window, coming to stand directly in front of her. "And you've known it didn't matter one damn iota. Why would you let it continue to matter to you?"

She shook her head, tempted to bare her soul but fighting not to. "But you don't understand how important it was for your family to accept me, to love me."

Dane stepped closer, looked into eyes that were fighting to keep tears at bay.

"Wasn't my love enough, Sienna? I'd told you countless time that you didn't marry my family, you married me. I'm not proud of the fact that my parents think too highly of themselves and our family name at times, but I've constantly told you it didn't matter. Why can't you believe me?"

When she didn't say anything, he sighed deeply. "You've been around people with money before. Do all of them act like my parents?"

She thought of her best friend's family. The Steeles. "No."

"Then what should that tell you? They're my parents. I know that they aren't close to being perfect, but I love them."

"And I never wanted to do anything to make you stop loving them."

He reached up and touched her chin. "And that's what this is about, isn't it? Why you filed for a divorce. You thought that you could."

Sienna angrily wiped at a tear she couldn't contain any longer. "I didn't ever want you to have to choose."

Dane's heart ached. Evidently she didn't know just how much he loved her. "There wouldn't have been a choice to make. You're my wife. I love you. I will always love you. When we married, we became one."

He leaned down and brushed a kiss on her cheek, then several. He wanted to devour her mouth, deepen the kiss and escalate it to a level he needed it to be, but he couldn't. He wouldn't. What they needed was to talk, to communicate to try and fix whatever was wrong with their marriage. He pulled back. It was hard when he heard her soft sigh, her heated moan.

He gave in briefly to temptation and tipped her chin up, and placed a kiss on her lips. "There's plenty of hot water still left in the tank," he said softly, stroking her chin. "Go ahead and take a shower before it gets completely dark, and then I'll take one."

He continued to stroke her chin when he added, "Then what I want is for us to do something we should have done months ago, Sienna. I want us to sit down and talk. And I mean to really talk. Regain that level of communication we once had. And what I need to know more than anything is whether my love will ever be just enough for you."

Chapter 12

You're my wife. I love you. I will always love you. When we married, we became one.

Dane's words flowed through Sienna's mind as she stepped into the shower, causing a warm, fuzzy, glowing feeling to seep through her pores. Hope flared within her although she didn't want it to. She hadn't wanted to end her marriage, but when things had begun to get worse between her and Dane, she'd finally decided to take her in-laws' suggestion and get out of their son's life.

Even after three years of seeing how happy she and Dane were together, they still couldn't look beyond her past. They saw her as a nobody, a person who had married their son for his money. She had offered to sign a prenuptial before the wedding and Dane had scoffed at the suggestion, refusing to even draw one up. But still, his parents had made it known each time they saw her just how much they resented the marriage.

And no matter how many times Dane had stood up to them and had put them in their place regarding her, it would only be a matter of time before they resorted to their old ways again, though never in the presence of their son. Maybe Dane was right, and all she'd had to do was tell his parents off once and for all and that would be the end of it, but she never could find the courage to do it.

And what was so hilarious with the entire situation was that she had basically become a workaholic to become successful in her own right so they could see her as their son's equal in every way; and in trying to impress them she had alienated Dane to the point that eventually he would have gotten fed up and asked her for a divorce if she hadn't done so first.

After spending time under the spray of water, she stepped out of the shower, intent on making sure there was enough hot water left for Dane. She tried to put out of her mind the last time she had taken a shower in this stall, and how Dane had joined her in it.

Toweling off, she was grateful she still had some of her belongings at the cabin to sleep in. The last thing she needed was to parade around Dane half naked. Then they would never get any talking done.

She slipped into a T-shirt and a pair of sweatpants she found in one of the drawers. Dane wanted to talk. How could they have honest communication without getting into a discussion about his parents again? She crossed her arms, trying to ignore the chill she was beginning to feel in the air. In order to stay warm they would probably both have to sleep in front of the fireplace tonight. She didn't want to think about what the possibility of doing something like that meant.

While her cell phone still had life, she decided to let her best friend, Vanessa Steele, know that she wouldn't be returning to Charlotte tonight. Dane was right. Not everyone with money acted like his parents. The Steeles, owners of a huge manufacturing company in Charlotte, were just as wealthy as the Bradfords. But they were as down-to-earth as people could get, which proved that not everyone with a lot of money were snobs.

"Hello?"

"Van, it's Sienna."

"Sienna, I was just thinking about you. Did you make it back before that snowstorm hit?"

"No, I'm in the mountains, stranded."

"What! Do you want me to send my cousins to rescue you?"

Sienna smiled. Vanessa was talking about her four single male cousins, Chance, Sebastian, Morgan and Donovan Steele. Sienna had to admit that besides being handsome as sin, they were dependable to a fault. And of all people, she, Vanessa and Vanessa's two younger sisters, Taylor and Cheyenne, should know more than anyone since they had been notorious for getting into trouble while growing up and the brothers four had always been there to bail them out.

"No, I don't need your cousins to come and rescue me."

"What about Dane? You know how I feel about you divorcing him, Sienna. He's still legally your husband and I think I should let him know where you are and let him decide if he should—"

"Vanessa," Sienna interrupted. "You don't have to let Dane know anything. He's here, stranded with me."

Chapter 13

"How was your shower?" Dane asked Sienna when she returned to the living room a short while later.

"Great. Now it's your turn to indulge."

"Okay." Dane tried not to notice how the candlelight was flickering over Sienna's features, giving them an ethereal glow. He shoved his hands into the pockets of his jeans and for a long moment he stood there staring at her.

She lifted a brow. "What's wrong?"

"I was just thinking how incredibly beautiful you are."

Sienna breathed in deeply, trying to ignore the rush of sensations she felt from his words. "Thank you." Dane had always been a man who'd been free with his compliments. Being apart from him made her realize that was one of the things she missed, among many others.

"I'll be back in a little while," he said before leaving the room.

When he was gone, Sienna remembered the conversation she'd had with Vanessa earlier. Her best friend saw her and Dane being stranded together on the mountain as a twist of fate that Sienna should use to her advantage. Vanessa further thought that for once, Sienna should stand up to the elder Bradfords and not struggle to prove herself to them. Dane had accepted her as she was and now it was time for her to be satisfied and happy with that; after all, she wasn't married to his parents.

A part of Sienna knew that Vanessa was right, but she had been seeking love from others for so long that she hadn't been able to accept that Dane's love was all the love she needed. Before her shower he had asked if his love was enough and now she knew that it was. It was past time for her to acknowledge that fact and to let him know it.

Dane stepped out the shower and began toweling off. The bathroom carried Sienna's scent and the honeysuckle fragrance of the shower gel she enjoyed using.

Given their situation, he really should be worried what they would be faced with if the weather didn't let up in a couple of days with the little bit of food they had. But for now the thought of being stranded here with Sienna overrode all his concerns about that. In his heart, he truly believed they would manage to get through any given situation. Now he had the task of convincing her of that.

He glanced down at his left hand and studied his wedding band. Two weeks ago when he had come here for his pity party, he had taken it off in anger and thrown it in a drawer. It was only when he had returned to Charlotte that he realized he'd left it here in the cabin.

At first he had shrugged it off as having no significant meaning since he would be a divorced man in a month's time anyway, but every day he'd felt that a part of him was missing.

In addition to reminding him of Sienna's absence from his life, to Dane, his ring signified their love and the vows that they had made, and a part of him refused to give that up. That's what had driven him back here this weekend—to reclaim the one element of his marriage that he refused to part with yet. Something he felt was rightfully his.

It seemed his ring wasn't the only thing that was rightfully his that he would get the chance to reclaim. More than anything, he wanted his wife back.

Chapter 14

Dane walked into the living room and stopped in his tracks. Sienna sat in front of the fireplace, cross-legged, with a tray of cookies and two glasses of wine. He knew where the cookies had come from, but where the heck had she gotten the wine?

She must have heard him because she glanced over his way and smiled. At that moment he thought she was even more breathtaking than a rose in winter. She licked her lips and immediately he thought she was even more tempting than any decadent dessert.

He cleared his throat. "Where did the wine come from?"

She licked her lips again and his body responded in an unquestionable way. He hoped the candlelight was hiding the physical effect she was having on him. "I found it in one of the kitchen cabinets. I think it's the bottle that was left when we came here to celebrate our first anniversary."

His thoughts immediately remembered that weekend. She had packed a selection of sexy lingerie and he had enjoyed removing each and every piece. She had also given him, among other things, a beautiful gold watch with the inscription engraved, *The Great Dane*. He, in turn, had given her a lover's bracelet, which was similar to a diamond tennis bracelet except that each letter of her name was etched in six of the stones.

He could still remember the single tear that had fallen from her eye when he had placed it on her wrist. That had been a special time for them, memories he would always cherish. That knowledge tightened the love that surrounded his heart. More than anything, he was determined that they settle things this weekend. He needed to make her see that he was hers and she was his. For always.

His lips creased into a smile. "I see you've decided to share the cookies, after all," he said, crossing the room to her.

She chuckled as he dropped down on the floor beside her. "Either that or run the risk of you getting up during the night and eating them all." The firelight danced through the twists on her head, highlighting the medium brown coiled strands with golden flecks. He absolutely loved the natural looking hairstyle on her.

He lifted a dark brow. "Eating them all? Three boxes?"

Her smile grew soft. "Hey, you've been known to overindulge a few times."

He paused as heated memories consumed him, reminding him of those times he had overindulged, espe-

cially when it came to making love to her. He recalled
one weekend they had gone at it almost nonstop. If she
hadn't been on the pill there was no doubt in his mind
that that single weekend would have made him a daddy.
A very proud one, at that.

She handed him a glass of wine. "May I propose a
toast?"

His smile widened. "To what?"

"The return of the Beast from the East."

He switched his gaze from her to glance out the window. Even in the dark he could see the white flecks
coming down in droves. He looked back at her and
cocked a brow. "We have a reason to celebrate this bad
weather?"

She stared at him for a long moment, then said quietly, "Yes. The Beast is the reason we're stranded here
together, and even with our low rations of food, I can't
think of any other place I'd rather be…than here alone
with you."

Chapter 15

Dane stared at Sienna and the intensity of that gaze made her entire body tingle, her nerve endings steam. It was pretty much like the day they'd met, when he'd walked into his father's study. She had looked up, their gazes had connected and the seriousness in the dark irises that had locked with hers had changed her life forever. She had fallen in love with him then and there.

Dane didn't say anything for a long moment as he continued to look at her, and then he lifted his wine-glass and said huskily, "To the Beast…who brought me Beauty."

His words were like a sensuous stroke down her spine, and the void feeling she'd had during the past few months was slowly fading away. After the toast was made and they had both taken sips of their wine, Dane placed his glass aside and then relieved her of hers. He then slowly leaned forward and captured her mouth, tasting the wine, relishing her delectable flavor. How had she gone without this for six months? How had she survived? she wondered as his tongue devoured hers, battering deep in the heat of her mouth, licking and sucking as he wove his tongue in and out between teeth, gum and whatever wanted to serve as a barrier.

He suddenly pulled back and stared at her. A smile touched the corners of his lips. "I could keep going and going, but before we go any further we need to talk, determine what brought us to this point so it won't ever be allowed to happen again. I don't want us to ever let anything or anyone have power, more control over the vows we made three years ago."

Sienna nodded, thinking the way the firelight was dancing over his dark skin was sending an erotic frisson up her spine. "All right."

He stood. "I'll be right back."

Sienna lifted a brow, wondering where he was going and watched as he crossed the room to open the desk drawer. Like her, he had changed into a T-shirt and a pair of sweats, and as she watched him she found it difficult to breathe. He moved in such a manly way, each movement a display of fine muscles and limbs and how they worked together in graceful coordination, perfect precision. Watching him only knocked her hormones out of whack.

He returned moments later with pens and paper in hand. There was a serious expression on his face when he handed her a sheet of paper and a pen and kept the same for himself. "I want us to write down all the things we feel went wrong with our marriage, being honest to include everything. And then we'll discuss them."

She looked down at the pen and paper and then back at him. "You want me to write them down?"

"Yes, and I'll do the same."

Sienna nodded and watched as he began writing on his paper, wondering what he was jotting down. She leaned back and sighed, wondering if she could air their dirty laundry on paper, but it seemed he had no such qualms. Most couples sought the helpful guidance of marriage counselors when they found themselves in similar situations, but she hadn't given them that chance. But at this point, she would do anything to save her marriage.

So she began writing, being honest with herself and with him.

Chapter 16

Dane finished writing and glanced over at Sienna. She was still at it and had a serious expression on her features. He studied the contours of her face and his gaze dropped to her neck, and he noticed the thin gold chain. She was still wearing the heart pendant he'd given her as a wedding gift.

Deep down, Dane believed this little assignment was what they needed as the first step in repairing what had gone wrong in their marriage. Having things written down would make it easier to stay focused and not go off on a tangent. And it made one less likely to give in to the power of the mind, the wills and emotions. He wanted them to concentrate on those destructive elements and forces that had eroded away at what should have been a strong relationship.

She glanced up and met his gaze as she put the pen aside. She gave him a wry smile. "Okay, that's it."

He reached out and took her hand in his, tightening his hold on it when he saw a look of uncertainty on her face. "All right, what do you have?"

She gave him a sheepish grimace. "How about you going first?"

He gently squeezed her hand. "How about if we go together? I'll start off and then we'll alternate."

She nodded. "What if we have the same ones?"

"That will be okay. We'll talk about all of them." He picked up his piece of paper.

"First on my list is communication."

Sienna smiled ruefully. "It's first on mine, too. And I agree that we need to talk more, without arguing, not that you argued. I think you would hold stuff in when I made you upset instead of getting it out and speaking your mind."

Dane stared at her for a moment, then a smile touched his lips. "You're right, you know. I always had to plug in the last word and I did it because I knew it would piss you off."

"Well, stop doing it."

He grinned. "Okay. The next time I'll hang around for us to talk through things. But then you're going to have to make sure that you're available when we need to talk. You can't let anything, not even your job, get in the way of us communicating."

"Okay, I agree."

"Now, what's next on your list?" he asked.

She looked up at him and smiled. "Patience. I know you said that I don't have patience, but neither do you. But you used to."

Dane shook his head. "Yeah, I lost my patience when you did. I thought to myself, why should I be patient with you when you weren't doing the same with me? Sometimes I think you thought I enjoyed knowing you had a bad day or didn't make a sale, and that wasn't it at all. At some point what was suddenly important to you wasn't important to me anymore."

"And because of it, we both became detached," Sienna said softly.

"Yes, we did." He reached out and lifted her chin. "I promise to do a better job of being patient, Sienna."

"So will I, Dane."

They alternated, going down the list. They had a number of the same things on both lists and they discussed everything in detail, acknowledging their faults and what they could have done to make things better. They also discussed what they would do in the future to strengthen their marriage.

"That's all I have on my list," Dane said a while later. "Do you have anything else?"

Sienna's finger glided over her list. For a short while she thought about pretending she didn't have anything else, but they had agreed to be completely honest. They had definitely done so when they had discussed her spending more time at work than at home.

"So what's the last thing on your list, Sienna? What do you see as one of the things that went wrong with our marriage?"

She lifted her chin and met his gaze and said, "My inability to stand up to your parents."

He looked at her with deep, dark eyes. "Okay, then. Let's talk about that."

Chapter 17

Dane waited patiently for Sienna to begin talking and gently rubbed the backside of her hand while doing so. He'd known the issue of his parents had always been a challenge to her. Over the years, he had tried to make her see that how the elder Bradfords felt didn't matter. What he failed to realize, accept and understand was that it *did* matter…to her.

She had grown up in a family without love for so long that when they married, she not only sought his love, but that of his family. Being accepted meant a lot to her, and her expectations of the Bradfords, given how they operated and their family history, were too high.

They weren't a close-knit bunch, never had been and never would be. His parents had allowed their own parents to decide their future, including who they married. When they had come of age, arranged marriages were the norm within the Bradfords' circle. His father had once confided to him one night after indulging in too many drinks that his mother had not been his choice for a wife. That hadn't surprised Dane, nor had it bothered him, since he would bet that his father probably hadn't been his mother's choice of a husband, either.

"I don't want to rehash the past, Dane," Sienna finally said softly, looking at the blaze in the fireplace instead of at him. "But something you said earlier tonight has made me think about a lot of things. You love your parents, but you've never hesitated in letting them know when you felt they were wrong, nor have you put up with their crap when it came to me."

She switched her gaze from the fire to him. "The problem is that *I* put up with their crap when it came to me. And you were right. I thought I had to actually prove something to them, show them I was worthy of you and your love. And I've spent the better part of a year and a half doing that and all it did was bring me closer and closer to losing you. I'm sure they've been walking around with big smiles on their faces since you got the divorce petition. But I refuse to let them be happy at my expense and my own heartbreak."

She scooted closer to Dane and splayed her hands against his chest. "It's time I became more assertive with your parents, Dane. Because it's not about them— it's about us. I refuse to let them make me feel unworthy any longer, because I am worthy to be loved by you. I don't have anything to prove. They either accept me as I am or not at all. The only person who matters anymore is you."

With his gaze holding hers, Dane lifted one of her hands off his chest and brought it to his lips, and placed a kiss on the palm. "I'm glad you've finally come to realize that, Sienna. And I wholeheartedly understand and agree. I was made to love you, and if my parents never accept that then it's their loss, not ours."

Tears constricted Sienna's throat and she swallowed deeply before she could find her voice to say, "I love you, Dane. I don't want the divorce. I never did. I want to belong to you and I want you to belong to me. I just want to make you happy."

"And I love you, too, Sienna, and I don't want the divorce, either. My life will be nothing without you being a part of it. I love you so much and I've missed you."

And with his heart pounding hard in his chest, he leaned over and captured her lips, intent on showing her just what he meant.

Chapter 18

This is homecoming, Sienna thought as she was quickly consumed by the hungry onslaught of Dane's kiss. All the hurt and anger she'd felt for six months was being replaced by passion of the most heated kind. All she could think about was the desire she was feeling being back in the arms of the man she loved and who loved her.

This was the type of communication she'd always loved, where she could share her thoughts, feelings and desires with Dane without uttering a single word. It was where their deepest emotions and what was in their inner hearts spoke for them, expressing things so eloquently and not leaving any room for misunderstandings.

He pulled back slightly, his lips hovering within inches of hers. He reached out and caressed her cheek, and as if she needed his taste again, her lips automatically parted. A slow, sensual acknowledgement of understanding tilted the corners of his mouth into a smile. Then he leaned closer and kissed her again, longer and harder, and the only thing she could do was to wrap her arms around him and silently thank God for reuniting her with this very special man.

Dane was hungry for the taste of his wife and at that moment, as his heart continued to pound relentlessly in his chest, he knew he had to make love to her, to show her in every way what she meant to him, had always meant to him and would always mean to him.

He pulled back slightly and the moisture that was left on her lips made his stomach clench. He leaned forward and licked them dry, or tried to, but her scent was driving him to do more. "Please let me make love to you, Sienna," he whispered, leaning down and resting his forehead against hers.

She leaned back and cupped his chin with her hand. "Oh, yes. I want you to make love to me, Dane. I've missed being with you so much I ache."

"Oh, baby, I love you." He pulled her closer, murmured the words in her twisted locks, kissed her cheek, her temple, her lips, and he cupped her buttocks, practically lifting her off the floor in the process. His breath came out harsh, ragged, as the chemistry between them sizzled. There was only one way to drench their fire.

He stretched out with her in front of the fireplace as he began removing her clothes and then his. Moments later, the blaze from the fire was a flickering light across their naked skin. And then he began kissing her all over, leaving no part of her untouched, determined to quench his hunger and his desire. He had missed the taste of her and was determined to be reacquainted in every way he could think of.

"Dane…"

Her tortured moan ignited the passion within him and he leaned forward to position his body over hers, letting his throbbing erection come to rest between her thighs, gently touching the entrance of her moist heat. He lifted his head to look down at her, wanting to see her expression the exact moment their bodies joined again.

Chapter 19

Sienna stared into Dane's eyes, the heat and passion she saw in them making her shiver. The love she recognized made her heart pound, and the desire she felt for him sent surges and surges of sensations through every part of her body, especially the area between her legs, making her thighs quiver.

"You're my everything, Sienna," he whispered as he began easing inside of her. His gaze was locked with hers as his voice came out in a husky tone. "I need you like I need air to breathe, water for thirst and food for nourishment. Oh, baby, my life has been so empty since you've been gone. I love and need you."

His words touched her and when he was embedded inside of her to the hilt, she arched her back, needing and wanting even more of him. She gripped his shoulders with her fingers as liquid fire seemed to flow to all parts of her body.

And at that moment she forgot everything—the Beast from the East, their limited supply of food and the fact they were stranded together in a cabin with barely enough heat. The only thing that registered in her mind was that they were together and expressing their love in a way that literally touched her soul.

He continued to stroke her, in and out, and with each powerful thrust into her body she moaned out his name and told him of her love. She was like a bow whose strings were being stretched to the limit each and every time he drove into her, and she met his thrusts with her own eager ones.

And then she felt it, the strength like a volcano erupting as he continued to stroke her to oblivion. Her body splintered into a thousand pieces as an orgasm ripped through her, almost snatching her breath away. And when she felt him buck, tighten his hold on her hips and thrust into her deeper, she knew that same powerful sensation had taken hold of him, as well.

"Sienna!"

He screamed her name and growled a couple of words that were incoherent to her ears. She tightened her arms around his neck, needing to be as close to him as she could get. She knew in her heart at that moment that things were going to be fine. She and Dane had proved that when it came to the power of love, it was never too late.

Sienna awoke the following morning naked, in front of the fireplace and cuddled in her husband's arms with a blanket covering them. After yawning, she raised her chin and glanced over at him and met his gaze head-on. The intensity in the dark eyes staring back at her shot heat through all parts of her body. She couldn't help but recall last night and how they had tried making up for all the time they had been apart.

"It's gone," Dane said softly, pulling her closer into his arms.

She lifted a brow. "What's gone?"

"The Beast."

She tilted her head to glance out the window and he was right. Although snow was still falling, it wasn't the violent blizzard that had been unleashed the day before. It was as if the weather had served the purpose it had come for and had made its exit. She smiled. Evidently, someone up there knew she and Dane's relationship was meant to be saved and had stepped in to salvage it.

She was about to say something when suddenly there was a loud pounding at the door. She and Dane looked at each other, wondering who would be paying them a visit to the cabin at this hour and in this weather.

Chapter 20

Sienna, like Dane, had quickly gotten dressed and was now staring at the four men who were standing in the doorway...those handsome Steele brothers. She smiled, shaking her head. Vanessa had evidently called her cousins to come rescue her, anyway.

"Vanessa called us," Chance Steele, the oldest of the pack, said by way of explanation. "It just so happened that we were only a couple of miles down the road at our own cabin." A smile touched his lips. "She was concerned that the two of you were here starving to death and asked us to share some of our rations."

"Thanks, guys," Dane said, gladly accepting the box Sebastian Steele was handing him. "Come on in. And although we've had plenty of heat to keep us warm, I have to admit our food supply was kind of low."

As soon as the four entered, all eyes went to Sienna.

Although the brothers knew Dane because their families sometimes ran in the same social circles, as well as the fact that Dane and Donovan Steele had graduated from high school the same year, she knew their main concern was for her. She had been their cousin Vanessa's best friend for years, and as a result they had sort of adopted her as their little cousin, as well.

"You okay?" Morgan Steele asked her, although Sienna knew she had to look fine; probably like a woman who'd been made love to all night, and she wasn't ashamed of that fact. After all, Dane *was* her husband. But the Steeles knew about her pending divorce, so she decided to end their worries.

She smiled and moved closer to Dane. He automatically wrapped his arms around her shoulders and brought her closer to his side. "Yes, I'm wonderful," she said, breaking the subtle tension she felt in the room. "Dane and I have decided we don't want a divorce and intend to stay together and make our marriage work."

The relieved smiles on the faces of the four men were priceless. "That's wonderful. We're happy for you," Donovan Steele said, grinning.

"We apologize if we interrupted anything, but you know Vanessa," Chance said, smiling. "She wouldn't let up. We would have come sooner but the bad weather kept us away."

"Your timing was perfect," Dane said, grinning. "We appreciate you even coming out now. I'm sure the roads weren't their best."

"No, but my new truck managed just fine," Sebastian said proudly. "Besides, we're going fishing later. We would invite you to join us, Dane, but I'm sure you can think of other ways you'd prefer to spend your time."

Dane smiled as he glanced down and met Sienna's gaze. "Oh, yeah, I can definitely think of a few."

The power had been restored and a couple of hours later, after eating a hefty breakfast of pancakes, sausage, grits and eggs, and drinking what Dane had to admit was the best coffee he'd had in a long time, Dane and Sienna were wrapped in each other's arms in the king-size bed. Sensations flowed through her just thinking about how they had ached and hungered for each other, and the fierceness of their lovemaking to fulfill that need and greed.

"Now will you tell me what brought you to the cabin?" Sienna asked, turning in Dane's arms and meeting his gaze.

"My wedding band." He then told her why he'd come to the cabin two weeks ago and how he'd left the ring behind. "It was as if without that ring on my finger, my connection to you was gone. I had to have it back so I came here for it."

Sienna nodded, understanding completely. That was one of the reasons she hadn't removed hers. Reaching out she cupped his stubble jaw in her hand and then leaned over and kissed him softly. "Together forever, Mr. Bradford."

Dane smiled. "Yes, Mrs. Bradford, together forever. We've proved that when it comes to true love, it's never too late."

* * * * *

*NEVER TOO LATE is part of
Brenda Jackson's*
FORGED OF STEELE *series.
Don't miss the latest story,
POSSESSED BY PASSION,
available March 2016
from
Kimani Romance.*

*And be sure to
pick up the other
stories in*
FORGED OF STEELE:

*SOLID SOUL
NIGHT HEAT
BEYOND TEMPTATION
RISKY PLEASURES
IRRESISTIBLE FORCES
INTIMATE SEDUCTION
HIDDEN PLEASURES
A STEELE FOR CHRISTMAS
PRIVATE ARRANGEMENTS*

Available from Kimani Romance.

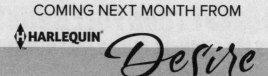

REQUEST YOUR FREE BOOKS!

2 FREE NOVELS PLUS 2 FREE GIFTS!

H HARLEQUIN®

Desire

ALWAYS POWERFUL, PASSIONATE AND PROVOCATIVE

YES! Please send me 2 FREE Harlequin® Desire novels and my 2 FREE gifts (gifts are worth about $10). After receiving them, if I don't wish to receive any more books, I can return the shipping statement marked "cancel." If I don't cancel, I will receive 6 brand-new novels every month and be billed just $4.55 per book in the U.S. or $5.24 per book in Canada. That's a savings of at least 13% off the cover price! It's quite a bargain! Shipping and handling is just 50¢ per book in the U.S. and 75¢ per book in Canada.* I understand that accepting the 2 free books and gifts places me under no obligation to buy anything. I can always return a shipment and cancel at any time. Even if I never buy another book, the two free books and gifts are mine to keep forever.

225/326 HDN GH2P

Name	(PLEASE PRINT)

Address	Apt. #

City	State/Prov.	Zip/Postal Code

Signature (if under 18, a parent or guardian must sign)

Mail to the **Reader Service:**
IN U.S.A.: P.O. Box 1867, Buffalo, NY 14240-1867
IN CANADA: P.O. Box 609, Fort Erie, Ontario L2A 5X3

Want to try two free books from another line?
Call 1-800-873-8635 or visit www.ReaderService.com.

* Terms and prices subject to change without notice. Prices do not include applicable taxes. Sales tax applicable in N.Y. Canadian residents will be charged applicable taxes. Offer not valid in Quebec. This offer is limited to one order per household. Not valid for current subscribers to Harlequin Desire books. All orders subject to credit approval. Credit or debit balances in a customer's account(s) may be offset by any other outstanding balance owed by or to the customer. Please allow 4 to 6 weeks for delivery. Offer available while quantities last.

Your Privacy—The Reader Service is committed to protecting your privacy. Our Privacy Policy is available online at www.ReaderService.com or upon request from the Reader Service.

We make a portion of our mailing list available to reputable third parties that offer products we believe may interest you. If you prefer that we not exchange your name with third parties, or if you wish to clarify or modify your communication preferences, please visit us at www.ReaderService.com/consumerschoice or write to us at Reader Service Preference Service, P.O. Box 9062, Buffalo, NY 14240-9062. Include your complete name and address.

HD15

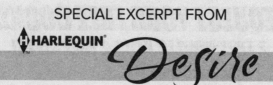
Claire looked completely panicked by the thought of Luca having access to her child.

Their child.

It seemed so wrong for him to have a child with a woman he'd never met. But now that he had a living, breathing daughter, he wasn't about to sit back and pretend it didn't happen. Eva was probably the only child he would ever have, and he'd already missed months of her life. That would not continue.

"We can and we will." Luca spoke up at last. "Eva is my daughter, and I've got the paternity test results to prove it. There's not a judge in the county of New York who won't grant me emergency visitation while we await our court date. They will say when and where and how often you have to give her to me."

Claire sat, her mouth agape at his words. "She's just a baby. She's only six months old. Why fight me for her just so you can hand her over to a nanny?"

Luca laughed at her presumptuous tone. "What makes you so certain I'll have a nanny for her?"

"You're a rich, powerful, unmarried businessman. You're better suited to run a corporation than to change a diaper. I'm willing to bet you don't have the first clue of how to care for an infant, much less the time."

Luca just shook his head and sat forward in his seat. "You know very little about me, *tesorino*, you've said so yourself, so don't presume anything about me."

Claire narrowed her gaze at him. She definitely didn't like him pushing her. And he was pushing her. Partially because he liked to see the fire in her eyes and the flush of her skin, and partially because it was necessary to get through to her.

Neither of them had asked for this to happen to them, but she needed to learn she wasn't in charge. They had to cooperate if this awkward situation was going to improve. He'd started off nice, politely requesting to see Eva, and he'd been flatly ignored. As each request was met with silence, he'd escalated the pressure. That's how they'd ended up here today. If she pushed him any further, he would start playing hardball. He didn't want to, but he would crush her like his restaurants' competitors.

"We can work together and play nice, or my lawyer here can make things very difficult for you. As he said, it's your choice."

"What are you suggesting, Mr. Moretti?" her lawyer asked.

"I'm suggesting we both take a little time away from our jobs and spend it together."

Don't miss
THE CEO'S UNEXPECTED CHILD
by Andrea Laurence, available March 2016 wherever
Harlequin® Desire books and ebooks are sold.

www.Harlequin.com

HDEXP0216

Looking for more wealthy bachelors? Fear not!
Be sure to collect these sexy reads from
Harlequin® Presents and Harlequin® Blaze!

A FORBIDDEN TEMPTATION
by Anne Mather

Jack Connolly isn't looking for a woman—
until he meets Grace Spencer! Trapped in a
fake relationship to safeguard her family,
Grace knows giving in to Jack would risk
everything she holds dear… But will she
surrender to the forbidden?

Available February 16, 2016

SWEET SEDUCTION
by Daire St. Denis

When Daisy Sinclair finds out the man she
spent the night with is her ex-husband's new
lawyer, she flips. Is Jamie Forsythe in on
helping steal her family bakery? Or was their
sweet seduction the real thing?

Available March 1, 2016